For Love...and Donuts

A Sophie Mays Novel

FOR LOVE...AND DONUTS

Text and Illustration Copyright © **2016 by Sophie Mays**

ISBN-13: 978-1539587347
ISBN-10: 1539587347

Publisher
Love Light Faith, LLC
400 NW 7th Avenue, Suite 825
Fort Lauderdale, FL 33302

To Julia and Caroline ~
You have each made this story and this dream possible
in your own uniquely amazing ways.
There are not enough donuts in the world to express
how much I appreciate you both.
From the bottom of my heart,

Thank You

TABLE OF CONTENTS

For Love...and Donuts

A Sweetwater Island Ferry Novel

Book 1

Chapter 1.

Virginia Ellis shoved the last bite of a Maple-glazed Pistachio donut into her mouth. Her eyes not able to break from the scene in front of her. The sight of Jason blatantly flirting with the slim, beautiful brunette sales assistant, his new hire at the TV station, felt like a hand gripping callously around her heart. She reached absently for her sparkling water and sipped. She was being melodramatic, she knew.

She had turned off the engine in her car when she'd pulled up, intending to jump out and scamper into Jason's work. Instead, she caught sight of the two fraternizing figures and froze up. As she sat in the stagnant car, too hypnotized to turn the AC back on, it ran through her head that this wasn't exactly the best decision on the cusp of summer during a record-breakingly hot year. The unseasonal afternoon temperature had soared into the eighties and she could feel the sweat forming on her brow, while both she and a dwindling half dozen donuts were melting into the car seats. Yet, she still couldn't manage to glance away from where Jason and the girl were standing. The whole scene played out like a romantic comedy, complete with doubled over laughter and animated chatting. The petite brunette was making a huge show of how endlessly funny Jason was being. Virginia knew Jason all too well, and while he was without a doubt charming, his jokes weren't known to have people rolling on the floor. Yes, this had all the makings of a classic romcom set up, except...except for the part where his heartbroken girlfriend sat less than twenty feet away feeling absolutely pathetic, frumpy and dejected, yet again. That part felt way less funny in real life.

Virginia may not have been destined to be a supermodel, or even the type of girl who commanded attention when she walked into a room, but she had always prided herself on being a kind person, an honest one, and someone who genuinely cared about people. She'd always felt comfortable with simply being herself. Unfortunately, she was pretty sure that her self-esteem was shot these days, and it had been for some time. And now here she was spying on her boyfriend. Last she checked, that was the ultimate cliche when it came to depicting an insecure girlfriend. She had always trusted Jason, never checked up on him. It was a point of pride with her that she wasn't "that kind of woman".

Now, as she watched him joke with his giggly co-worker, lightly touching her arm as they leaned against the wall of the building, obviously on a break, Virginia couldn't help but wonder if trusting him was naive.

Tearing her eyes away from the couple, she glanced to the passenger seat and fished around for another donut. She wished she didn't know what went into them. The creamy European butter and eye-averting amounts of sugar that she poured into each batch of oversized gourmet donuts made them insanely delicious, but wasn't doing much to support her yearly resolution of a healthy, waist-whittling diet. Most days, she happily baked her goods, fueled her tiny side business and partook in little more than a lick of the spatula when she finished the icing. On days like today, however, she found herself dipping heavily into her inventory like the weak, un-savvy drug dealers she always saw on Jason's TV shows. Those guys never fared well, and the comparison wasn't lost on her.

Jason leaned back against a waist-high cement barrier, stretching out his toned torso and apparently saying something else rip-roaringly witty. Her eyes glazed over, memories of seeing him in high school way before they ever started dating. For as long as she could remember, she had loved Jason. Sure, she'd had crushes on other boys, but from the moment she and Jason had started dating Senior year of in high school, she'd known they would be together forever. He was everything that a high school art student could have dreamt of: Captain of the baseball team, outgoing and popular, with dark hair, a chiseled jaw and piercing hazel eyes. She had always been slightly awkward in high school:

pretty but shy, an honor student interested in the visual arts, books, baking and little else. The fact that a boy like Jason bothered to look her way at all was a minor miracle as far as she was concerned. And when he kissed her for the first time at the homecoming dance, she knew that there would be no one else. She and Jason would live happily ever after.

And so they would. This was nothing. Men flirted with women all the time. It didn't mean anything. He always came home to her, in a manner of speaking. Jason had told her a thousand times that he respected her decision not to live together until they were married, even if that came at a cost. I mean, he'd also made it known that he wanted to live together and that he thought it was a little silly and old fashioned not to. He wanted to do all the things that couples do when they live together, but somehow he'd still stayed with her when she just couldn't give in to that.

She was raised as a good Christian girl in a good Christian household. Even though she hadn't been to church in a few months, even though she hadn't really prayed in weeks, some things still didn't change. And living with a man she wasn't married to was still going to be one of them.

A tiny, horrible voice in her head whispered that maybe, just maybe, that was the reason he was chatting up the pretty young assistant. Maybe, if she gave him all the things modern men expected to get from their girlfriends, Jason wouldn't be looking for it elsewhere.

Virginia popped the end of the next donut in her mouth, huffed and dismissed the voice immediately. He said he was willing to do whatever she thought was best and hadn't given her any reason to think otherwise. Besides, even though this girl was young and thin and beautiful, something that he alluded to Virginia not being anymore, she couldn't help but notice that she looked quite a lot like Virginia had looked several years before. In fact, whenever she saw Jason flirting, anyone could easily see that the girls resembled her in her younger years. That was a good sign, right?

She had to admit that between working two jobs to help put Jason through graduate school for his Marketing degree, starting the side business catering small-batch donuts, teaching art to school kids, and the long hours she had put in to make it all work, it had taken a bit of a toll on her. It made sense that he flirted with other girls. Over the last few years, too much stress and too little exercise had caused her thin figure to fill out significantly. She wasn't what anyone would call overweight, but no one would stop short of calling her pleasantly chubby, or maybe "soft" on a good day.

Suddenly her phone beeped with a text. "So, what did the will say?"

It was from Jason. "Thought you were going to text me when you were done and stop by." Virginia hesitated, swallowing the lump in her throat. "Yeah, be there soon." She fought back the sinking feeling in her stomach.

Besides, he'd been under stress, too. And stress affected people in different ways. She couldn't blame him for looking. It said a lot about him that he had stayed with her despite all they had been through. She opened the car door, took in a refreshing breath of the late Spring air, and wiped at the rims of her eyes clean. She got out of the car and walked into the building.

"Hey, babe!" Jason exclaimed casually, peering out at her from behind his computer screen, as she approached his section of the relatively open-concept sales office. "Did you bring us some donuts?" He threw a smirk to the pretty sales assistant who was seated at the front desk. The girl gave Virginia a demure, almost embarrassed smile as Virginia walked past her, before turning away and pretending to focus on something on her computer screen.

"Um, yeah," she shook her head absentmindedly, "I did bring some, but I forgot them in the car. Sorry. I can go out and get them in a sec."

Jason chuckled, "That's my honors student," he said playfully. "Always on top of things."

Virginia smiled at his easy tone, his flirtation with the sales assistant nearly forgotten.

"Well, I've had a lot on my mind today," she said smiling with a mock defensive tone.

"Oh yeah. What did you find out about the will?" he asked leaning forward in his chair and lowering his voice.

He was talking, of course, about her aunt

Emily's Last Will and Testament. Virginia had gotten a phone call the previous week from her late aunt's attorney saying that she was named in her aunt's will.

To say that Jason was curious about the will was an understatement.

"This could be the answer to those student loans you've been worrying about!" he had said at dinner one night. "And, if it's enough money, who knows? We might even be able to talk about getting married finally!" Talk of their wedding was a double-edged sword for Virginia. On one hand, what girl wouldn't want to talk endlessly about the magical day when she would marry her lifelong love. But Jason had grand plans for their wedding which far outweighed her own, and the finances to fund it had become an insurmountable hurdle that kept pushing it back and back and back. She wouldn't have cared if they got married with just a few close friends at the park down the street. Jason however, had dreams of a show-stoppingly opulent affair. He went on to tell her about some of the more impressive wedding venues he'd heard about, causing her the choke at the associated price tags he quoted.

Jason was one of those people who just looked like he should have money. He carried himself like a Kennedy, and it was no secret between them that he aspired to live a luxury lifestyle one day. In the meantime, he did all he could to create the pretense to the outside world that he was already well off. But the reality of the situation was that the last few years had been lean.

They had decided some time ago that any money they made should be considered theirs, plural. And the idea had been that it made the most sense for Virginia to support Jason while he was building a solid career foundation, with the thought that it would all be an investment in their combined future. So she had done all she could for the last few years to make it so he could get ahead by focusing on school and not worrying as much about working. Thankfully Jason finally had a job as an Account Executive, which brought in a decent salary, but it wasn't enough to cover the massive student debt he'd built up in addition to his everyday life expenses. So Virginia had been slowly paying down his school loans every month, not leaving a whole lot of money for other things. And while Jason dreamed of having money, he admittedly wasn't the best at managing it, and always seemed to be living slightly beyond his means. Which was why he was so anxious to hear about the money Virginia was soon to come into. It was also why Virginia was so hesitant to give him the news.

"Well, it's not what we thought it would be," she said with a small sigh. Her heart constricted when Jason's face fell.

"You mean it's less than what we expected?" he asked.

"Not...not exactly," she said. "It's...kind of complicated..."

"Now you're making me nervous," he said with a little smile and a chuckle, clearly attempting to make light of the nerves he felt.

"It's just...it's not money," she said.

"What do you mean?" he asked. "Is it like an antique table or something?"

"Bigger than that," Virginia said. "She left me the old summer cottage on Sweetwater Island."

"A house?" he asked. His eyes squinting in surprise.

"I haven't been there in a few years. Not since Aunt Emily moved to the city," Virginia admitted, "but it's the same one I used to go to every summer when I was little."

He leaned back in his chair nodding in

recognition. Then he bit his lip and furrowed his brow. Virginia knew this look well. It was the one Jason always got when he was thinking seriously about something.

"Is it for you and Samantha to share?"

"No, Sam was given our aunt's jewelry collection. She's been obsessed with it her entire life, and Aunt Emily always told her it would be hers one day," Virginia reported on her sister's inheritance.

Jason paused a minute before asking, "But, you said it's a nice house, right? Like a Victorian sort of place? Any chance we could...you know...sell it?"

Virginia felt her chest clench.

"Sell it?" she asked.

"Yeah," he said, "I mean, we just...we really need the money you know?"

"I know," Virginia said slowly. "I just. I hadn't thought about-"

"Jason?"

The pretty sales assistant swiveled in her chair towards them.

"I could use your help with this sales packet. I mean...if you're not busy," she said, throwing a slightly guilty look at Virginia.

This look brought the scene she'd witnessed outside the building back to the front of Virginia's mind. The shame and anger she'd felt sitting in that car, watching them, came back along with it.

"Look," Virginia said to Jason, a little more harshly than she'd intended. "You're clearly busy. Just...come over for dinner tonight and we'll talk about it. Ok?"

Jason blinked and looked slightly taken aback.

"Ok," he said slowly. "Honey, are you feeling ok?"

Realizing how harsh she'd sounded, Virginia took a deep breath and told herself to calm down.

"Yeah," she said. "I'm fine. I just...I've got a ton of donut orders to fill today. I guess I'm a little stressed."

Jason nodded in understanding.

"Make sure you don't work yourself too hard," he said gently, putting a hand over hers and squeezing it sympathetically.

Virginia smiled at his touch, the anger and shame almost completely gone.

"Same goes for you," she said. "I'll bring those donuts in. Then I'll...see you tonight."

"See you tonight, hun," he said.

She quickly walked out to the car, grabbed the donuts and brought them in to Jason, who's joking mood had returned.

"I see you already sampled a few," he teased within earshot of his co-workers. "You know, that's how the weak drug dealers always get taken out on TV." He raised his hands in a dramatic gesture. "You never do your own drugs! You don't have enough self-control! The drugs will control you… Aughhh…" He cracked up at his reenactment, "I should've been in movies, not selling advertising for them..". She forced a light laugh and walked out.

As she took the familiar drive back to the home she shared with her sister Samantha, she tried pointlessly to push the earlier scene she'd witnessed out of her mind. You're being paranoid she repeated to herself. You know he loves you. No matter how often he looks at other girls, he would never cheat on you. That's why he was so excited about the will, wasn't it? He wants to marry you!

Even so, the paranoid, insecure feelings nagging at the back of her mind wouldn't leave her alone. And she knew they wouldn't go away until she let them out. Tonight when Jason came over for dinner she would have to talk to him about it.

She didn't know how she was going to go

about it; confrontation had never been her strong suit. But, she did know that her mind would never settle until she did.

Chapter 2.

"Is pretty boy coming over?" Samantha asked offhandedly as she bounced down the steps of the little duplex she and Virginia shared just outside of Seattle.

Virginia rolled her eyes. Her sprightly, flaxen-haired sister, despite being two years Virginia's junior, had always been overprotective of her.

After their parents had passed away, Samantha had insisted on moving in with

Virginia. Of course, Virginia understood why and it was an instinct she shared. Both girls had been left enough in a trust fund for each of them to have their own place, even in a market as expensive as Seattle, yet they agreed that they would prefer to live together. They had been raised well, but humbly, and the trustee, an old friend of their father who served as his longtime financial manager, sat down with the girls to make a plan for the money in a way that would keep with their parents' wishes to have the girls grow up responsibly. He encouraged them to let him invest the bulk of the money, allowing them to live off the interest and dividends, though they had a standing policy that the girls could ask for a larger amount of money for special things, like the purchase of their duplex. At this point, the amount they received wasn't significant, which was why Samantha worked a part time job at night and went to college during the day. It was also why Virginia had started her baking business, and also worked part time as a floating art teacher for the nearby school district. Each girl was encouraged to try to build their own self-sufficient wealth above and beyond the trust.

Still, at the end of the day, Virginia knew the other reason Samantha moved in was because she didn't trust her sister in the big, mean city.

Sam had never liked or trusted any of Virginia's boyfriends. And that included Jason, who she still referred to as 'pretty boy'.

"You know Jason always comes over on Wednesday nights," Virginia said.

"I still don't understand why you always have to cook for him," Samantha said. "And I don't understand why you can never go over to his place."

"He only has a little efficiency," Virginia said. "The kitchen's too small there to do any cooking. Besides, you're always at work when he comes over."

Samantha worked the night shift at an upscale 24-hour fitness center. This meant that she was often asleep during the morning when Virginia was baking for her donut business and she was away at night when Jason would often come over for dinner.

Even so, Samantha looked at her older sister skeptically.

"Come on, Sam," Virginia said with a hint of playful frustration. "You know Jason's not going anywhere. You're going to have to get used to him."

"I am used to him," Sam said. "Doesn't mean I have to like him."

Virginia rolled her eyes as Sam made her way into the kitchen and opened the fridge. She pulled out a cup of yogurt and nothing else.

Now it was Virginia's turn to look at her

little sister skeptically.

"You're going to need more than that for an eight-hour shift," Virginia said.

"You know I'm on a diet," Samantha said with an eye roll. This was a point of contention between Virginia and her sister. Samantha, who was short, blonde and incredibly skinny, was always convinced that she needed to lose weight. And Virginia was convinced that, if her sister didn't eat more, Samantha was going to fade away before her eyes.

"Look, just...for my sake. Take a banana with you to work or something."

"Do we have bananas?" Sam asked.

"Just bought some," Virginia answered. Sam smiled at her sister.

"I never thought I'd see the day you would willingly purchase fruit," Sam said.

"It's for a new donut recipe I'm trying out," Virginia answered.

Samantha heaved a playful sigh. "Well, it's

a start anyway," she said.

Samantha sat on top of the kitchen counter as Virginia prepared the chicken breast she was making for that evening's dinner. Samantha, meanwhile, entertained her with the always amusing late-night antics she encountered at work. While her acting chops probably wouldn't win her an Oscar, Sam's reenactments of the gym clients were always performed with gusto, whether they were the young, overworked corporate-types stumbling in late at night to try and sleep in the locker rooms before hustling back to their nearby offices, or groups of riled up guys rolling in when the bars close because a bet got out of hand as to who could bench press the most.

Though the stories in and of themselves were hilarious, Virginia couldn't help but be glad she had not followed in her sister's footsteps, job-wise.

Just as Virginia was putting the chicken in

the oven and Samantha was preparing to leave for work, the lock clicked in the front door.

"That's probably Jason," Virginia said wiping her hands on a dish towel and moving towards the front door. Before she left the kitchen, she turned back to her sister.

"Be nice," she warned Samantha.

Sam pursed her lips and narrowed her eyes.

"I will as long as he doesn't act like a jerk," Samantha said.

Virginia, realizing she wasn't going to get a better promise out of her little sister, walked to the front door which swung open as she approached.

"Hey babe," he said walking in and giving her a kiss. Virginia smiled at Jason as she pulled back and noticed a six pack of beer in his hand.

"Glad you remembered," she said.

Two nights before he'd complained loudly

about Virginia not having booze in the house. She'd told him that her sister wouldn't allow it. So, if he wanted beer, he'd have to bring it himself.

"I still don't get why your sister doesn't like alcohol," he said following Virginia into the kitchen.

"It's part of her diet," Virginia said evenly.

"Well, a diet that doesn't make room for beer isn't any diet I'd want to be on," Jason answered with a laugh.

It happened that just at that moment, they rounded the corner to the kitchen where Samantha was waiting, her arms crossed and frowning at Jason.

Virginia cursed inwardly. She could feel the tension coming off her sister before anyone spoke. Apparently, Jason was oblivious to it.

"Oh, hey Sam," he said moving past both Virginia and Samantha and taking a seat at the kitchen table. "Didn't know you were here."

"You don't say," Samantha said through gritted teeth. She turned to him and gave him one more glare which Jason did not seem to have noticed before she turned her gaze back to Virginia.

"I've gotta go. See you tomorrow morning," Samantha said.

"See you then," Virginia said, feeling a faint pang of relief at the thought that her sister and her boyfriend would not be in the same room for long.

With one more sneer at an oblivious Jason, Samantha grabbed the banana Virginia had made her take and stalked towards the front door. Jason waited until it had closed completely before he spoke again.

"She still doesn't like me," he said. Virginia's guilt surged as she realized that Jason apparently wasn't as unaware of Sam's agitation as she'd thought.

"Sam's just protective," Virginia said.

"Yeah, I understood that when we were first dating," Jason said. "But...I mean...you'd think she'd have warmed up by now."

"There are very few people Samantha actually likes," Virginia said. "The fact that she tolerates you should make you feel all warm and fuzzy inside."

Jason let out a full buoyant laugh. Virginia couldn't help but smile fondly at the sound. She'd always loved the sound of his rich, deep, full-throated laugh. It was one of the things that had first made her fall in love with him.

"I guess I should be grateful," he said. "Who knows, one day Sam and I might even have a civil conversation. If I'm really lucky, she may just smile at me."

"It has been known to happen," Virginia said dryly.

"I'll tell you one thing," Jason said grabbing a beer from his six pack and cracking it open. "I won't hold my breath until it does."

He offered a beer to Virginia who declined. She filled a glass with sparkling water instead and sat at the table with Jason.

They talked about safe, simple things. Things like his day at work. The new orders she'd gotten in for her donut catering business. What the traffic had been like for him on the way over to her house.

She knew Jason wouldn't bring up what he really wanted to talk about until dinner was on the table. Just like she wouldn't bring up what she needed to talk about until Jason was full and satisfied.

As per usual, Jason's point of discussion came up first. Virginia had just placed his chicken onto the bed of brown rice on his plate and was doing the same with her own when Jason spoke.

"So, have you thought any more about what you want to do about the house?" he asked.

Virginia pursed her lips as she set the serving in front of him and sat down. She hesitantly took a fork full of food.

"I don't know." Not wanting to elaborate she took a larger bite of her dinner.

"Well, think about it," Jason said. "I mean, we couldn't really do much with a run down house. I've already got a place. And, you're happy living here, aren't you?"

"Yeah," she answered, though it was slightly non-committal. While she knew how lucky she was to get a duplex in the city, and while she enjoyed her sister's company, she couldn't pretend that she hadn't often thought longingly of the little town where her Aunt's old cottage was.

A small town surrounded by woods and the scent of pine. Shops where her Aunt knew each of the owners. Walking trails brimming with wildlife and flowers. The scent of the sea filling the air when you sat on a rock at the coast. It was the sort of place she'd always imagined herself living when she grew up. As a child, and even a teenager, it had been her dream home.

Of course, that was before she'd met Jason. Before she'd realized that he was a city boy through and through.

"Besides, it's not like we don't need the money," he said. "We've still got all my student loans to pay off. Not to mention credit card debt. Money from the house could help us take care of all that."

"I know," Virginia said.

And she did. She and Jason had discussed all their economic difficulties in great detail. And, she couldn't pretend that it wouldn't be a relief to get rid of some of that burden.

Still, the idea of just giving the house up was not particularly enticing. It was almost like giving away a beloved family heirloom or a treasured childhood toy. A piece of her childhood would disappear along with the house. It would be a small piece, but a piece none the less.

"If you know that," Jason said, "then, what's the problem?"

"It's...it's sentimental, I guess," she said. She knew the moment she said it that Jason wouldn't really understand. Both his parents were still alive. He'd never really lost anyone close to him before.

Even so, when she looked at him, he gave her a sympathetic smile and reached over to touch her hand.

"Babe, I know you loved your Aunt," he said. "And your Aunt knew you loved her. That's why she gave you the house. She wanted you to use it in the best way you could."

"But, did she really expect me to...sell it?" Virginia asked.

"She didn't leave any instructions, did she?

Nothing that said you had to use it any specific way?" he asked.

"Well...no," Virginia answered honestly. Jason smiled almost triumphantly as he patted Virginia's hand before taking his away.

"There you go!" he said. "If your Aunt knew how much we needed the money, I'm sure she would've understood."

Virginia gave a reluctant nod. Truth be told, Jason had a point. Aunt Emily was always trying to take care of Virginia and her sister, Sam. Her Aunt had no children of her own and she had sort of adopted her nieces and nephews.

Aunt Emily was forever telling Virginia that if she needed money or a loan not to hesitate to ask. Virginia had always turned down the offers. She felt guilty about asking for money, even though she knew her Aunt Emily could afford to lend it.

Perhaps this was Aunt Emily's way of

helping Virginia out financially. Something Virginia couldn't refuse.

"It's...it's going to take some work," Virginia said reluctantly. Putting in her last defense against the sale of her childhood haunt.

"I know it's old," Jason said. "But, I've got a little money saved up. I'm sure you do, too. How much do you think it'll take?"

"I'm not sure, honestly," Virginia said. "I haven't been there in a few years. Not since Aunt Emily moved out."

The cottage had been abandoned since Aunt Emily became sick and moved to an apartment in the city to be near the hospital. She knew even then that there was no point in having someone take care of the house. She knew even then that she would never return.

"Well, then, we should probably make an appointment with that real estate agent. Get down there and check it out," Jason said finishing the last bite of his meat.

Virginia nodded but a guilty pang filled her stomach once more. Maybe it was the idea of consulting a real estate agent. Even though Virginia already had someone she liked that she and her sister had used to purchase the duplex, the idea of consulting her about her Aunt's cottage just seemed so...official.

"Hey," she heard Jason say gently as she looked up from her plate. "This is the right thing to do. Nobody can blame you for fixing the house up and selling it to someone who'll use it."

"I...I guess I know that," Virginia said.

Jason set his fork down and looked at her thoughtfully.

"How about this?" he said finally. "We won't make any decisions until we actually see the place with the relator. If we can't get much money for it, even after it's been renovated, we won't sell. Does that sound ok?"

Virginia looked at him, hesitating for a moment.

He reached across the table again, put his hand over hers and gave it a squeeze. She looked into his eyes and the soft, sympathetic smile he gave her made them sparkle.

Her heart melted and the guilty feeling dissipated.

"Yeah. That's fair," she said finally. "Thanks."

With another squeeze of her hand, he stood up from the table. He walked around until he stood at her side and put an arm around her shoulder.

"I know you've had a rough day," he said. "So, why don't you pick the movie tonight? Anything you want. Even one of those silly romantic comedies. I promise I won't complain."

Virginia gave a surprised snicker and looked up at him. He rarely let her pick what they watched after dinner. Try as she might to get into his shows, the truth was that their tastes tended to differ widely.

"You're sure about that?" she asked.

"I think, after what you've been through, the least I can do is stomach some girly tv," he said with a teasing smile.

"Ok," she answered, "but no takebacks."

"No takebacks," he said, "I promise."

He leaned down and placed a gentle kiss on her temple. She closed her eyes as his warm lips and the scent of his spicy cologne filled her nostrils. His, strong steady arm curled around her shoulders and she couldn't help but smile.

A moment later, he pulled away.

"I'll go into the living room and get the TV set up while you clean up in here," he said.

With a quick and charming wink thrown her way, he left the kitchen.

Virginia's smile remained on her face even

as she stood to gather the plates and put them in the dishwasher. True, a better offer from Jason would have been to do, or at the very least, help with the mountain of dishes. But, she knew with him, baby steps were to be praised. Plus, giving up precious control of the tv remote was a big baby step.

That's why, as she basked in the memory of his soft kiss on her temple, she forgot all about the discussion she'd wanted to have with him about his assistant…

Chapter 3.

Virginia's car gently idled as she sat in the line queued up for the ferry which would take them to Sweetwater Island. She flinched in pain as she bit down, realizing that she was absentmindedly chewing on her thumbnail. The plan was for Jason to park in the commuter lot, then hop into her car with her so that they could go over and meet with the real estate agent, Amanda. Jason had to work, so they figured Virginia could get a jump on the car line by going early. Her phone beeped, and she glanced in her side window to see if she could see Jason walking toward her car. She would be much calmer once he was with her. Knowing that they were in this together made her feel more confident and at ease about the whole thing. A quick daydream of the moment she would finally look into Jason's eyes over a perfect bouquet of creamy white lilies and say "I do" brought a dreamy smile to her face.

Focusing back on reality, she scooped up her phone to check the message. Jason probably couldn't find her car in the line up.

She scanned across the words, "Sorry, I can't make it. Something came up with work. Tell me what you find out."

Her jaw clenched and she rolled her eyes, cursing him for the fourth time that day.

She knew that wasn't really fair; it was a Wednesday morning, after all. He'd told her he might have trouble getting off work, even though he'd put in for a half day.

Suddenly, Virginia felt even more uncertain about the outing than she had that morning. She was already nervous about seeing the beautiful summer home that had filled her childhood, likely neglected and in ill repair. But, having to do it alone, or nearly alone, was even worse.

Still, she knew there was nothing to be done about it.

She drove onto the ferry's containment area, got out of the car and made her way up to the top deck.

A deep and hollow horn bellowed through the air and she felt the initial jolt of the boat moving. Closing her eyes, she could feel the wind blowing gracefully across her face. The wisps of her feathery brown hair whipped into her eyes and fluttered across her cheeks. While the sensation was a little annoying, it also reminded her of the first time she had stepped foot on the boat as a child. She'd laughed when her hair had flown into her face back then.

She remembered the thrill of excitement her much younger self had felt riding this same old ferry boat so many years ago. Once her father had made his first million, her parents had started taking summer trips to Europe, just the two of them. Samantha and Virginia had gotten to spend those times vacationing with Aunt Emily on their magical island. She smiled at the memory. Even now, there was something magical about getting on the boat and leaving your cares behind on the mainland. She hadn't spent nearly enough time out here in the last few years.

A squawking gull above the stern reprimanded her for her failure to visit. Virginia smiled up in apology to the hovering bird.

The ferry was one of only two ways in which to get to Sweetwater Island and it was by far the most efficient. The land road towards the island took over an hour from almost the same spot as the ferry and if the rickety old bridge that led to the island was out, it could take much longer.

The ferry took only twenty minutes. Virginia was surprised to find herself so disappointed when the boat pulled to a stop. The hollow, nervous feeling which had disappeared almost completely on the ferry ride over, returned as she got back into her car.

She drove down the pothole filled road into the main town of Sweetwater and tried to remember what Jason had said. They didn't have to make any decisions until they'd talked to Amanda. And if the house wasn't worth much of anything, even after renovations, they might not sell it at all.

As Virginia drove past the lovely Victorian cottages at the outskirts of the town, with their pale purple shutters, steepled roofs, and mysterious towers springing up from their sides, she found herself hoping that the house would not be worth anything. That meant that she would be able to keep it, she reasoned to herself.

Of course, she felt more than a bit guilty when she thought about that. After all, shouldn't she want to get them out of debt? Didn't she want Jason to be able to pay off his student loans? Didn't she want to have enough money to get married?

Besides, Jason was right. What were they going to do with a house so far from the city? They both worked in Seattle, and if they lived on the Island, commuting would be hell. Even with Virginia's inheritance, there was no possible way they could afford to keep a "summer" house.

No. If it was at all possible, the cottage would have to be sold.

Even so, when Virginia pulled into Sweetwater's small downtown, a nostalgic smile crept across her face.

Driving down the main street, she passed the old ice cream parlor. Aunt Emily would take them there on Saturdays when they'd been good all week. To tell the truth, even when they hadn't been as good as they could have been, they would still make the trip to the ice cream shop. Aunt Emily couldn't seem to help spoiling the girls.

Just across from the ice cream parlor was another treat. The second-hand bookshop where they would go on Sunday afternoons after church. That was where Virginia had found an entire set of Nancy Drew mysteries and her little sister had fallen in love with Gossip Girl.

Next to the bookstore was the Supermart.

Though it wasn't as exciting as the other places, Virginia and Sam always felt very grown up when Aunt Emily asked them to walk down to the Supermart alone and get her the ingredients for supper, or occasionally, a frozen pizza.

Virginia looked to the shop next to the Supermart and felt a jolt of disappointment when she saw a shiny new electronics store in place of where the old video rental shop used to be. She supposed she should have expected that. Since streaming had come down the pike, everything happened over wifi now. Even in remote places like this, there were no video stores left.

Still, as everything else had been the same, she naively thought it would be there; an antiquated building frozen in time to remind her of Friday nights with her aunt and sister when they would rent three movies, usually silly comedies, and watch them back to back.

She turned her attention away from the offending electronics store and headed down the main street and up the small hill that led to the cottage. As soon as the last shop was passed, Virginia entered into what looked like desolate woodland. There was nothing on the hill next to the cottage except tall pine trees on either side of a barely drivable dirt road.

Even so, the woods she drove through were every bit as filled with memories as the main street she had left behind. Her eyes quickly found the tree with extra low limbs that she used to climb. Closer to the cottage, she spied the twin rocks facing the town that she and her sister used to sit on.

Then, just beyond the rocks was the house itself.

Virginia nearly gasped when her eyes landed on it. She had expected the house to look exactly as she remembered it. When she was young, the quaint, two-story wooden home looked like something out of a fairytale. The gables of the roof were painted white and the window shutters were pink. There was a high, pointed roof and a light turquoise blue door highlighting white scalloped shingles covering the facade.

Now, the paint on the once beautiful blue door had been peeled so thoroughly that the ugly brown color of the original door showed through. The white gables were so overrun with pollen from the surrounding trees that they now sported a kind of sickly greenish-yellow color. The pristine little window shutters were hanging off their hinges, and the once blushing pink color was molded with dust and grime.

Had it not been for the familiar pointed roof still standing tall amidst the forest of pine trees, Virginia would not have believed this was the same cheery house she came to every summer as a girl.

Trying as best she could to stifle the sinking feeling in her heart at seeing the house in this state, she pulled up to the side of the grassy hill that functioned as the driveway and parked next to a white Chevy Cruiser.

A tall, older woman with plump, rosy cheeks and short, curly, brightly dyed red hair, stood next to the car talking to someone on her cell phone.

Virginia's mood lifted a bit at the sight of the real estate agent. It was nice to know that Amanda Benson was exactly as she remembered her from two years before, even if the house was very different.

"Look, honey, I know your brother took your toy, but you have to learn to share," Virginia heard her saying in a high pitched voice to someone who definitely had to be a child on the other end of the phone. Amanda turned and gave Virginia an apologetic smile. Virginia waved, in turn, telling her it was all right.

"Ok," Amanda continued to the mysterious child on the phone. "Do you promise you're going to be good? Ok. Remember, you can't break a promise. I love you, too. Bye bye."

With a heavy sigh, Amanda clicked the end button on the phone and turned fully to Virginia.

"Sorry about that," Amanda said. "My daughter's husband was transferred overseas and she's gone over to find a new houes and whatnot. So the grandkids are staying with me until they get things settled."

"How old are they?" Virginia asked.

"Lilly's four," she said. "That's who I was trying to talk some sense into on the phone. And Mikey is two."

Virginia gave her a sympathetic grimace. She knew Amanda was in her late fifties. What's more, her husband had passed away ten years before. It was hard to imagine her taking care of two young kids on her own.

"That can't be easy," Virginia said.

"Well, I've got a lot of help," Amanda answered. "My neighbor has a little girl around Lilly's age. So she takes the kids when I go out to show houses. Luckily I'm not working at the office anymore so...I can make it work."

Though she was attempting to toss the issue aside, Virginia could easily see the worry lines on the woman's face. Those hadn't been there two years ago when Amanda had sold Sam and Virginia the duplex.

"Well," Amanda said blatantly attempting to change the subject. "Shall we take a look at the house?"

"I guess we should," Virginia said reluctantly. "I haven't been here in what feels like forever. I didn't realize how much it had been let go."

"Oh, don't let that get you down," Amanda

said in her light and genuinely cheerful voice. "Remember, I've seen a lot of houses that don't look like much at first. Some of them have become my favorite projects! It's amazing what can happen when you put just a little time and a lot of love into a place."

Despite Amanda's reassurance, as they entered through the sad, peeling door, Virginia couldn't help but think that this house needed much more than time and love.

They stepped into the front walkway and Virginia was immediately assaulted by another flood of memories mixed with a heavy layer of dust.

The grime on the outside of the house was nearly as bad on the inside. Even so, the warm wood floor of the front walkway was the same as she remembered it being when she was young.

When she looked to her right, towards the living room, Aunt Emily's old, tufted mauve couch was still there, too. It was moth-eaten now and looked significantly dusty. But when Virginia caught sight of it, she could vividly remember sitting right beside her aunt as she read to Virginia and her little sister.

Aunt Emily was a great fan of children's literature, and when the girls were small, she would read all of her favorites to them. These included The Wind in the Willows, Alice in Wonderland and nearly every book by Roald Dahl in print.

"The carpet will have to be torn up, of course," Amanda said as they moved into the living room. This brought Virginia's attention to the horribly stained carpeting beneath her feet. It had been white at one point but was now a sort of brownish color.

"Aunt Emily always talked about putting in wood floors anyway," Virginia said. "I think she'd like it if we changed that."

She moved through the old living room,

coughing slightly at the dust that came up from the surfaces as she did so. Moving to the window, she stopped when she saw an intricate spider's web hanging from the corner.

"Oh, don't worry about that," Amanda said following her gaze. "There'll be a lot of spider webs in here. Nothing a good dusting won't fix."

Virginia was not worried. In fact, she couldn't help but smile as she watched the light hit the small strands, causing the colors in the web to shift and fold into one another.

Her Aunt Emily had always loved spider webs. When they found one, the girls were never permitted to ruin it if they could help it.

"Spider webs are good luck," she insisted. "If you see one, especially in your house, it means that something really good is about to happen."

Of course, Virginia had no idea where this legend had come from. In fact, she was almost certain that Aunt Emily had made it up. But still to this day, it had instilled in Virginia a sort of respect for both spiders and the webs they spun.

"There's a lot more that'll need changing of course," Amanda said as she led Virginia through a small archway which separated the living room from the family room and connected kitchen.

As Amanda continued the tour, Virginia could see that she was right. Her Aunt's antique furniture, most of which was still sitting in the old house, was dust filled and molding and would have to be replaced.

Amanda also suggested retiling the kitchen and bathrooms as the flooring had become too dirty to be salvaged.

Virginia didn't mind this so much. She knew, before she'd passed away, Aunt Emily had talked about making changes to the house. In fact, she'd been talking about it for years. She just couldn't seem to set aside the time to do it.

Now, Virginia thought, even if they did have to sell it, making the changes her Aunt had always wanted would give her a slight sense of peace. Like a last tribute to Aunt Emily. It wasn't until Amanda took her to see the bedrooms that a bittersweet sadness filled Virginia's chest.

"I definitely think we'll want to update the rooms," Amanda said opening the door to the second largest bedroom to the right of the small hall off the kitchen.

Virginia let out a small gasp when the door opened. This bedroom was the one Virginia had slept in every summer when she came to the cottage. And it was almost perfectly preserved.

Her stuffed animals who had made their home here still sat on the small day bed just next to the window. That day bed was still decorated with an old, stained, purple comforter with a lace frill on the bottom.

To the right of the bed stood her bookshelf. It still housed her, now very dusty, complete collection of Nancy Drew mystery novels.

"I think we could turn this into a nice office or guest room if you-"

"I don't think I'll change much in here," Virginia said in a rush. Amanda turned to look at her surprised. It was the first time Virginia had protested any suggested change.

Realizing how forceful she'd sounded, Virginia felt her face go red and she looked at the floor as she explained herself.

"It's just...this was my old bedroom. I liked it this way and...I think...I mean if we just change a few things...some other kid might like it too."

When she looked up, she was pleased to see that Amanda was giving her a sympathetic smile.

"I understand," she said giving her arm a small pat. "You probably won't want to change it completely. You lose a lot of memories that way."

They continued the tour upstairs through the other bedrooms and bathroom where Amanda suggested similar updates to the draperies and flooring. Finally, they made it to the back deck. Or rather, the entranceway to the back deck.

"The wood rot's too bad for us to risk going out on the deck right now," Amanda said. "That'll be the first thing we'll have to replace when you start working on the house. It's a safety issue."

Virginia nodded, looking out past the rotted back deck. An old tire swing swung in the light summer breeze that she and Samantha had put up their third summer there. It was strange to see it looking so empty. Just as strange as it was to hear the backyard so quiet. Virginia's memories of this yard had always been filled with loud peals of children's laughter.

"Well," Amanda said closing the door and jolting Virginia back to the present. "That's about all I can show you. There's the attic too, of course, but, that's as bad as the back deck. We definitely wouldn't want you falling through the floor up there."

Amanda gave a good-hearted chuckle. Virginia smiled and gave a polite nod, her mind whirling from the tour of her past.

"Just from what I can see now, the foundation of the cottage is actually very good," Amanda said. "As we say in the industry, it has good bones. But, it'll need a lot of work."

"How much do you think we'd have to put in to get it back in shape?" Virginia asked.

"It won't be cheap," Amanda said. "I'd say somewhere in the fifty to one hundred thousand dollar range."

"You're right. That's not cheap!" Virginia said, taken aback. When she remembered all the debt she still had to pay off from Jason's schooling, she wondered how such a huge sum, taken out all at once, was going to affect her bank account.

Maybe it wouldn't be worth it to sell the house with all the money they'd have to put into it. Virginia couldn't help but feel oddly hopeful at the thought.

"But," Amanda continued, "If you do get it fixed up, I could sell it for two or even three times what you put into it, plus what the property itself is worth."

"Really?" Virginia asked. Trying to sound excited even as she felt the disappointment wash over her.

"Oh, yes," Amanda said eagerly. "As I said, this house has a great structure. Not to mention, this market has really taken off. Lot's of people are moving from the city out to the islands."

"So, you think we'd be able to make a profit on it?" Virginia asked, once again, trying to keep the disappointment out of her voice.

"I'm positive," Amanda said. "That is if you're willing to put the money for the repairs in?"

Amanda looked at Virginia expectantly, awaiting her answer. Virginia knew what that answer had to be.

She'd told Jason that, if Amanda said they could make a profit on the house, she would put up the money for repairs. Virginia knew she had the money in her trust fund. And while it would take a chunk out of the inheritance she'd gotten from her dad, it wouldn't bankrupt her completely.

"Yeah," Virginia said. "Yeah, we can do that."

"Perfect," Amanda said excitedly as she led

the way back to the family room, past the living room and out to the front yard.

"Now, we'll just need to find you a good contractor," Amanda said just before they reached their cars.

She reached into her purse and rooted around for a card index. Shuffling through it, she came back with two crisp, clear and very professional looking business cards.

"Now, these two are excellent companies. But, I should warn you, their prices tend to run a little higher than normal. Are you willing to go over one hundred thousand if it comes down to it?" she asked hesitantly handing Virginia the cards.

Virginia bit her lip. She knew that she could just spare the hundred thousand by tapping into her highly guarded savings account, and applied what she could from her meager teaching and baking incomes. If she paid the bare minimum on Jason's loan and was careful with her own spending for the next few months, she could make it work. Anything over that, however, would become a good deal more complicated.

"I...I don't know," she answered.

Amanda looked at her thoughtfully. It was a moment before the older woman began shuffling in her purse again.

"Well, if you want something a little cheaper but still reliable," Amanda said pulling out another card. "You might try this new company."

She handed Virginia a small and much more plain business card. This one had no colorful logo. Simply the words Solid Rock Contractors printed in large, bold letters. Beneath these was the name Tristan McPherson along with a phone number and email address.

"Strictly speaking, my real estate company hasn't used him before," Amanda said. "But, he goes to my church, and I've hired him for some repairs around my own house. He's very reliable and very affordably priced. Not to mention, he's wonderful with my grandkids. They call him Uncle Tristan now. But, I don't suppose that matters much to you."

Virginia looked up at the woman and smiled.

"I don't know," she said half teasing. "They always say that dogs and little kids have a better sense about people than adults do. If a dog or a young child likes someone, I'm more inclined to trust him."

Amanda's smile widened.

"That's what I've always said," she answered.

They said goodbye and Virginia promised to let Amanda know when she'd settled on a contractor.

As she drove back through the town, Virginia tried her best not to look at the familiar shops, storefronts, and homes. The guilty feeling she had at deciding to sell the place that she'd loved so much as a child was still stubbornly beating in her chest.

At least, she reasoned, as she made it back to the dock for the ferry, I can fix up the house first. Which means I'm sure I'll get to come up and see it again a few times before it's sold.

Yes, she told herself, a proper goodbye was all she needed. She felt increasingly certain that, with time, she would feel ready to say goodbye.

Chapter 4.

"Absolutely not!" Jason said. His voice was so loud that Virginia had to move the cell phone away from her ear.

She'd just called both of the first places Amanda had recommended. When she'd talked to Jason about their options the night before, he wanted to go with one of the first two companies, mostly because the real estate company had used them for home renovations before. Plus, they looked more professional than the third, admittedly newer option.

Virginia had warned Jason that the quotes might be a little high. He said he still wanted her to check them out first. Now that she'd gotten the quotes, one of which was just at one hundred thousand and one of which was a good amount over, Jason was audibly unhappy.

"You didn't see the place, Jason," Virginia said. "It needs a lot of work."

"The realtor said the work is just aesthetic, right?" Jason asked. "I mean, they don't need to fix the plumbing or anything. How much overhead could there be putting in a hardwood floor and a few tiles?"

"Amanda said they might be a little pricey," Virginia countered.

"Well, she was right about that," Jason huffed. "I don't want to see you lose another chunk of your trust fund to a bunch of highway robbers."

"Well," Virginia said, "we do have that third option."

"The church guy?" Jason asked a slightly derisive note in his voice.

"Yeah, Amanda said he would probably be more affordable."

"But will he be as good?" Jason asked.

"Amanda's used him on her own house," she answered. "She says he does good work and he's really reliable."

She didn't feel the need to mention that he was good with kids. She knew Jason wouldn't exactly appreciate the significance of that. Men never seemed to. There was a pause over the phone during which Virginia was sure she could hear Jason thinking.

"Ok," he said finally. "Go ahead and give him a call."

They said their goodbyes and I love you's before Virginia hung up. She fished the third card out of her purse and stared at it for a good few minutes.

At first glance, she could see why Jason had been reluctant to try this company. Besides the fact that the card was very plain, the email address was Gmail rather than a company server. The phone number was doubtlessly a personal cell phone as well.

But, Virginia knew from her dad that sometimes, small businesses did the best work. And those small businesses could often grow beyond even the founder's wildest dreams.

With that in mind, she sat on her couch and dialed the number on the card. The phone rang twice before a voice on the other end answered.

"Solid Rock Contracting, this is Tristan."

The musical, tenor voice implied a much younger man than Virginia had been expecting. The way Amanda had described him, reliable, good with the grandkids, she had expected a kindly older gentleman.

"Hi," she said a little timidly. "I was hoping to get a quote for some work I need done on a house?"

"Oh, you must be Virginia!" The man said cheerfully. "Amanda said you might be calling."

"Yeah," Virginia said, feeling some relief. She was happy that she wouldn't have to explain the whole situation to Tristan. "Did she tell you about the work that needed to be done on the house?"

"Most of it," he said. "I just need to be filled in on a couple of the details."

They discussed the work Virginia and Amanda had talked about wanting to do. Amanda had already told Tristan about the outer deck and the attic. Virginia filled him in on the new wood floors she wanted to have put in and the new tiles she wanted in the bathroom.

"I know you'll probably need new furniture to show the house, too," Tristan said. "I've got a furniture guy I work with. Would you like me to put a call in to him?"

"Oh, don't worry about that," Virginia said hastily. "I can take care of the decorating and stuff on my own."

Truth be told, that was the one aspect of this job Virginia was looking forward to. It had been a long while since she had put any of her artistic sense to use outside of her teaching job and it would be fun to have something other than baking to keep her busy during the summer.

"Ok," Tristan said. "If you change your mind about that, let me know." Virginia thought he sounded skeptical but reminded herself that this was to be expected. Guys who made their living working on houses always had their doubts about amateurs doing a professional's job.

In the end, Tristan gave her a quote for the entire project that was a good deal lower than what both of the other contractors had offered.

"I'll have to talk to my boyfriend," Virginia said. "But, it sounds like we'll probably go with you."

"Great," Tristan said sounding much more excited than either of the guys from the larger company. She wondered if, perhaps, this was the largest job his small company had ever gotten.

"Ok. I'll send you an email tonight with confirmation and some times when we could go and check out the house. You can let me know which of them will work for you."

"Sounds perfect," he said. "Can't wait to get started."

As soon as she and Tristan said their goodbyes, Virginia ended the call and immediately sent a text to Jason. She knew his break would be over by now and texting was the only way she was likely to get a hold of him.

She texted him the quote Tristan had given her. It was only a few minutes before her phone buzzed with a text in reply.

"Ok. Let's go with him."

As soon as she read the text a wave of relief flowed through her. Virginia shot off the promised confirmation email to Tristan with several suggestions of meeting times within the next week.

As she put her phone away and moved from the living room back into the kitchen where a cooled batch donuts awaited icing, she realized that the sense of dread she felt about the house had gone away completely. In fact, after talking to Tristan, she felt lighter than she had in weeks.

Perhaps that was why it did not surprise her at all to see a shining spider web in the corner of her kitchen window, even though she swore it had not been there when she'd left the kitchen less than two hours before.

She simply smiled at the little design, wondering if it was a sign of Aunt Emily's blessing.

With a happy sigh, she decided that it was just that.

Chapter 5.

The second ferry ride in a week was just as fraught with the mixture of anxiety, calm, excitement and disappointment as the first had been.

She felt an exhilarating burst of energy at going back to Sweetwater again. The town's charm had not been lost on her the last time she came out. And this time, she'd planned to spend some time perusing around the little shops. Maybe even get an ice cream from the shop where she and her sister used to go.

As she exited the ferry and drove back down the single road towards the town, her brain shot into overdrive. She couldn't help but stress about the money she was spending on the renovations for the cottage. Even though Amanda had assured her that she could sell the house for twice as much if not more, nothing was certain and it was a substantial amount for anyone, most particularly someone with an income like hers.

After all, the sale price depended on what the market was like, whether luck was on their side and, perhaps most of all, on how good this contractor was.

This would be Virginia's first meeting with Tristan McPherson and she supposed Jason's doubts about this newer and less tested company had rubbed off on her. Even though Jason had agreed to hire Tristan's company, he still wasn't one hundred percent sold on them.

"I mean, sure he's cheap," Jason said only one day after he had agreed to Tristan's quote, "but that might come with a cost all its own."

Of course, when Virginia reminded Jason that he'd agreed to hire Tristan's company, Jason had defended himself by saying that he was just 'playing devil's advocate'. Trying to make sure they were ready for every possible scenario.

Though she knew Jason meant well, his form of 'disaster preparation' had put her on edge.

Of course, some of Jason's fears might have been put to rest if he'd been able to come out with her today and meet Tristan for himself.

That was where Virginia's disappointment came into play. She'd once again invited him to come out to the island with her, and once again, he'd backed out at the last minute. Another pressing matter had come up at work.

Though Virginia knew she shouldn't

complain, she still wished he would double-check things at work before agreeing to come with her in the first place. Although knowing that she would have to go alone three days ago when she'd made the appointment would still have been a little disappointing, it would have been nothing compared to the hurt she felt when, the morning of, he texted her to tell her 'Sorry. Can't make it after all.'

Trying to take Jason off her mind, she glanced out the window as she drove through town once more. This time, she noticed the small shop that sold antique furniture. She made a mental note to spend some time in there after the meeting. She could find some nice pieces to put in the house once it was finished.

She passed the rest of the trip up the hill pleasantly painting a picture in her mind of what she wanted each room in the little cottage to look like when she had finished with it.

The anxiety didn't come back until the car crawled to a stop at the top of the hill just outside the front door of the house. She saw an unfamiliar blue pick-up truck parked outside that wasn't the gleaming, logo-encrusted company vehicle she had imagined that the other guys probably drove.

Its bed was piled with wood, lumber and what looked like several other tools. Obviously the contractor was already here, but there was no sign of him near the truck.

She got out of her car and moved curiously from her parking spot around to one side of the house.

"Hello?" she called out. No answer.

She padded around the side garden, now overgrown with weeds, hoping to see any sign of human life. She didn't find any.

Virginia wondered, suddenly, if the contractor had gotten tired of waiting for her and somehow left. But she dismissed this almost immediately. She was only five minutes late. Plus, between the state of his truck and his easy voice over the phone, she surmised that Mr. Tristan Mcpherson was not particularly finicky about time constraints.

She moved through the tall grass shaded by the high pine trees to the back of the house. That was where she found him.

A slim male figure bent over a piece of old wood on the weathered back deck. Even though his back was turned to her, she could sense an air of deep concentration emanating from him. From out of his red flannel overshirt, Virginia saw a sun-stained hand move out and touch the dark, ruined wood with an odd sense of reverence.

The action was so charged with feeling that Virginia did not feel quite right about interrupting it. Still, she knew she had to. She hadn't planned on the tour taking too long, since she still wanted time to look at furniture in the town shops.

Feeling slightly guilty, she cleared her throat.

She was surprised when this elicited no response. The man simply turned to the side, his eyes still focused on the wood in front of him. Now that she could see his face more clearly, Virginia was forced to admit that he was much better looking than she'd expected him to be.

When she thought about handymen who owned small businesses, an image of large, usually bearded men with leathery skin and slight beer bellies came to mind.

This man was not particularly brawny or burly or bearded. He was lean and strong, but had an almost boyish air about him. His light brown hair was tousled and his chin was completely clean shaven, not to mention very defined. The hand he still ran across the splintered wood was not at all aged or leathery. It was fair, with a light tan from the gentle Washington sun and looked very smooth.

He was now moving his feet along with the motion of his hand. Moving along the edge of the deck as though trying to memorize it.

She would have to try again to get his attention.

"Tristan?" she asked, making her voice as loud as she dared. The young man whirled around to face her. His bright blue eyes startled. When they finally took stock of her, a pink blush rose up in his light cheeks. She thought she could make out some very light freckles scattered across them too. It made him look quite cute, all things considered.

"You must be Virginia," he said sounding the tiniest bit self-conscious. "Sorry, I was just-"

"Don't apologize," Virginia said with what

she hoped was an encouraging smile. "I was the one who was late."

He gave her a sheepish smile in return and moved forward to shake her hand.

"Nice to meet you," he said in the same light tenor voice she had heard on the phone. She put her hand out to shake his and thought to herself that his hand was just as smooth and warm as it had looked when he'd been examining the wood.

"You too," she said with a blush of her own. She released her hand from his as quickly as she could and brought her attention back to the deck.

"I see you've started looking at the deck. Hope it didn't scare you off."

"Not at all!" Tristan said. "To tell the truth, I've wanted to work on one of these old, Victorian cottages since I started my business. Before this, all I got were small jobs on modern suburban houses. Not nearly as much fun."

"Probably not as much effort either," Virginia countered.

Tristan gave a vague nod in her direction before moving back to the deck. Once more he put his hand out to touch a piece of rotting pine.

"You don't see a lot of places with the original wood still in place," he said. His voice was impressed, almost awestruck. "It's amazing that it's still here at all!"

"Judging by the rot, there's probably a reason most people don't keep the original," she replied.

"Oh, that part can be replaced easily enough," he said with a dismissive wave of his hand and moving back over to the deck. He took a rolling measurement tape out of his back pocket and put it up to the front steps of the deck.

"I'd still like to use local wood if you wouldn't mind," he said. "It would be nice to keep as true to the original look and feel of the place as possible."

"I wouldn't mind at all," she said feeling genuinely impressed as she watched him carefully measure the step. He stood up and pulled a small notebook from his side pocket. She had a sudden feeling that, once again, he hadn't heard her.

"In fact, I'd like to keep the original look of the house as much as possible," she said slightly louder hoping that would get his attention. It did; he turned around and looked at her blinking once more in surprise.

"Really?" he asked. "No modernizing? No bringin' it into the twenty-first century?'"

His look of surprise had turned to slight skepticism as he looked her up and down. Virginia realized that she was wearing her "business" clothes today. She had a meeting with one of the clients she catered donuts for after this and she always made a point to dress well when she went to those.

However, she realized that when Tristan looked at her in her pencil skirt, gauzy navy and white blouse and wedge heels, he saw something that didn't sit well with him. And what's more, his prejudice didn't sit well with her.

"You sound surprised," she said. "Did you think I'd want to change everything?"

"Most people do these days," he said unashamedly. "Especially interior designers. Amateur or otherwise."

Now, she recognized the tone he'd used with her on the phone when she'd told him that she would take care of the interior decorating. He'd seemingly made assumptions about her based on that interaction, that he was not too willing to part with.

"Well, I guess I'm not most people," she said, frowning at him for the first time. "And I'm definitely not just some amateur interior designer. This house is special to me. I spent every summer here from the time I was six to the time I was sixteen. Is it so amazing that I'd want to keep it the way I remember it?"

He blinked and she was slightly satisfied when she saw another light pink blush come into his cheeks.

"I'm sorry. I didn't mean...I mean, I shouldn't have...it's just, I thought..."

He mumbled as he looked down at his feet. His shamed face and half finished apologies were enough to make Virginia feel sorry she had spoken to him so harshly.

"Don't worry about it," she offered up, giving him a small smile. "Honest mistake. Now, would you like to see the rest of the house? Or is the deck enough for you to go on?"

He looked up and gave a small smile at her joke.

"No, I'd love to see the rest of it," he said.

"If the deck's anything to go by, I'm going to love this project."

That was also surprising, Virginia thought, as she led him around the side and back to the front door. This contractor was perhaps the first person she'd ever met who could get excited about a deck filled with rotting wood. Original or not.

She was even more surprised that his enthusiasm continued as they moved through the rest of the house. He didn't seem to be able to help gushing over the unpainted woodwork on the walls.

"You're Aunt was so smart not to paint this over," he said. "Most people do. But, really, the wood is meant to show through. It looks so much better this way!"

He was equally thrilled about the fireplace and the window panes. "She even kept the original fireplace tile! That'll be perfect."

He did have ideas and suggestions for

changes. Both he and Virginia agreed that they wanted to open up the kitchen a bit and, of course, that the bathrooms would need to be re-tiled and spruced up.

Overall though, he seemed determined to remain true to the original character of the house. He seemed to bounce around from room to room, measuring and openly admiring the craftsmanship and woodwork. The way most guys got about football or video games, Tristan, apparently, got about old houses.

As they finished the tour, Virginia found all her doubts about Tristan's lack of experience had melted away. He clearly appreciated this house as much as she did. That was enough to let her know that she was leaving it in good hands.

"So, do you think you'll be able to have it ready by September?" Virginia asked. "I know Amanda said that having it ready to show by fall would be best."

"Oh, no problem," Tristan said eagerly. "I've got most of the materials I'll need already. The rest I can get pretty easily. I'll bring my assistant out here to get started tomorrow morning."

"That soon?" Virginia asked, once again surprised.

"The sooner the better," Tristan said. "Especially if we want to get it finished by fall. Though, truthfully, it's mostly 'cause I can't wait to get started here." He grinned as he threw her a quick side glance.

"Glad to hear it," Virginia said. "I'll be over sometimes to see how things are going."

"That's fine," Tristan said, though she noted some skepticism had returned slightly to his voice, as though he were an artist who did not like the idea of an outsider intruding on his work. "Just be sure to call me first. I don't want there to be any accidents if you were walking around looking for us and didn't know where to watch your step. That can sometimes happen when outsiders visit a site."

Once again, the way he said 'outsiders' didn't quite sit well with Virginia. It was as though he saw her as an "other". Someone who didn't really appreciate what he was going to do with the house.

"Trust me," Virginia said, her tone a tad defensive. "I know my way around construction sites. And, I'll be sure to call."

"Ok then," Tristan said. This time he didn't seem to feel the need or desire to apologize for unintentionally offending her. He simply stared back at her, his wide blue eyes meeting her green ones with a small smirk on his lips as though she'd said something funny.

Virginia didn't say anything more, but gave him a quizzical look as she led the way back out the front door and down the steps to their cars.

"Here's the key," she said fishing the large, antique key out of her purse. It was the one her aunt had given her when she was young. It had an ornate heart fashioned into the handle and Virginia loved it.

Even though she had decided that she trusted Tristan with the house, she still felt a pang of reluctance at handing the key over.

He must have seen the hesitance in her face when he reached for the key because his expression changed when he took hold of it. He regarded her deeply as though he was trying to read what was written on her face.

As he eased the key out of her hand, a knowing expression came over him. It was as though he finally understood why she was so hesitant.

"I'll take good care of it," he said earnestly, "I promise."

"Please do," she said. "This place is...very

special to me."

He gave her a wide, empathetic smile which she couldn't help but return.

"I can see why," he said. "It's in good hands."

"Thank you," she answered. Virginia felt a silent sigh release in her chest. She was relieved that, at last, someone understood her reluctance to part with this magical place.

They said their goodbyes and Virginia watched as Tristan got into his truck and headed down the hill. The feeling of relief remained as she got into her own car, and in fact, it followed her all the way into town as she browsed for furniture.

As she looked at antique wooden wardrobes and bed frames, she found herself wondering if Tristan would approve of these pieces. Would they be 'original' or 'authentic' enough for him?

She didn't quite know the answer. But, the

questions made her smile.

Chapter 6.

"Are you baking for pretty boy again?" Samantha asked, wandering into the kitchen, yawning with her school books under her arm. It was almost eleven thirty in the morning and Sam had just woken up from her too-short seven-to-eleven nap before going to her afternoon class.

"If you mean Jason," Virginia answered wearily. "No, I'm not. He's gone on a business trip down to Portland for a couple of days."

"Is he taking that hot sales assistant with him?" Samantha asked wryly. Virginia, unable to keep entirely quiet about the dalliance she had witnessed outside the television station had mentioned it to her sister. Something she was now beginning to regret. It had given Samantha even more reason to hate Jason.

"Sales assistants don't go on business trips, so that you know," Virginia said tossing her second batch of donuts in the oven and grabbing the icing for the first. "And really, you need to lay off Jason about that," she continued, her back turned towards her sister. "It was probably nothing."

Samantha gave a snort of disbelief but, thankfully, said nothing more. Virginia heard Sam move to the refrigerator as she focused on filling a pastry with the new banana cream she'd promised herself she would try.

"So, if you're not baking for your

boyfriend, who are those for?" Sam asked from behind Virginia. She turned to see Samantha setting down her books on the kitchen island while coffee brewed on the counter behind her.

"Well, the second batch will be for an order I need to ship out by tomorrow," Virginia said. "This first batch is kind of experimental. I've been playing with some new flavors."

"I hope you don't expect to test them out on me!" Sam said vehemently. Virginia rolled her eyes at her sister.

"I know that trying to get you to eat a donut would be a waste of time," Virginia said. "I thought I'd take them up to the renovation team working on the house. I should check on their progress anyway."

Samantha stared at her sister with an oddly pointed look. Virginia turned back around to the donuts, a sense of guilt washing over her. Though she wasn't sure just why.

"You know, I still can't believe you're selling it," Samantha said.

"I asked you about it," Virginia said. "You told me you didn't really care, remember?"

"That's true," Sam said. "I don't particularly. I mean, I loved going there when I was a kid but, that's really not the sort of place I'd like going now. I'd rather just keep the memories. But...you're not like that."

"Not like what?" Virginia asked hoping her voice sounded light enough that it didn't make her sister suspicious.

She heard Samantha heave a sigh.

"You know what I mean," Samantha said. "You love quaint little island towns and antique shops and old Victorian houses. I mean, you're happier when we go out to the country camping than I've ever seen you in the city. Getting rid of what should be your dream house just isn't...like you!"

Virginia recognized the tone in her sister's

voice and knew she would have to give her some kind of explanation. She turned to look at Samantha with a sigh of her own.

"Look, Sam, you know money's kind of tight right now," Virginia said. "Besides, Jason and I really want to get married and we can't do that until we get some extra income."

Sam's skeptical look didn't go away. She stared Virginia down as though trying to see through her. Virginia, unsure what else to do, stared right back. Finally, with a shrug of her shoulders, Sam turned back towards the coffee, grabbed hold of the carafe and poured herself a cup.

"Whatever you say," Sam said in a resigned tone. "I know getting you to give up on pretty boy is like you trying to get me to eat donuts."

Virginia gave a half-hearted laugh and continued decorating the rest of the batch.

Sam and Virginia ended up leaving the

house at the same time. Sam set off for class at the university only two blocks away while Virginia, donuts in hand, got in her car and made her way to the ferry.

When she arrived at the loading dock, she looked at the long line of cars waiting to drive onto the boat. The lunch rush, she supposed. Early morning, noon and around five o'clock in the evening were the worst times for taking the ferry out to the island. She cursed herself for not remembering that.

Just looking at the huge line of cars made her feel a restless urge to get out of her driver's seat and move. Glancing sideways at the nearly empty parking lot beside the loading dock, she made a snap decision.

Turning her steering wheel right, she moved herself away from the car line and towards the parking lot. She would go on the ferry as a foot passenger. It wasn't a long walk from the bay to the cottage and no one could argue that she didn't need the exercise.

Grabbing the box of donuts beside her, she got out of the car and joined the much shorter line of foot passengers onto the boat.

The ferry ride seemed much shorter this time around than it had in the past. In no time, she had set her feet on the island and was moving up the hill the back way to the cottage.

The little walking trail didn't go through the small downtown of Sweetwater. Instead, it wound through the tall pines and oaks taking her along the picturesque hillsides where she had a view of the sparkling blue ocean.

She, Aunt Emily and her sister had walked this path to the ferry many times in the past. Virginia remembered coming back from shopping trips in Seattle with bags of clothes or toys in hand. She and her sister happily racing one another to abstract markers like the tree with the weird shaped trunk or the huge boulder at the top of the hill.

Every whiff of pine and blow of the ocean breeze seemed to take Virginia back there. To that much simpler time when she did not have to think about how much money was left in her bank accounts, or whether or not her boyfriend would really propose once they had the cash from the house.

Finally, she reached the cottage and could see Tristan's truck parked in the expected spot just beside the front door. As she moved closer, she could hear the sound of pounding as well as a raised voice swearing oaths at a particular wall in the house.

She knocked on the door though she was sure it couldn't be heard over both the hammering and one-sided argument. She tried the doorknob and to her surprise, it opened immediately.

"Hello?" she asked hesitantly. "Tristan?"

"Oh! Come on you stupid wall!" The sound of his voice exclaimed, quite audibly from the kitchen. She moved cautiously through the front hallway which was now littered with tools and a hefty layer of sawdust. Finally, she entered the kitchen where Tristan was facing a wall, large hammer in hand, with no sign of an assistant anywhere.

"Hello?" she asked again.

He gave a small start and turned around. His eyes widened when he caught sight of her. His flannel shirt and jeans were covered in exactly the same heavy layer of dust as the hallway outside and sweat was dripping down his brow.

"Virginia!" he said. "I...I didn't know you were coming by today."

His cheeks colored in what she had to admit was a very cute shade of pink. Clearly, he was embarrassed to be seen in such a state, though Virginia couldn't think why. It was no more than she'd expected.

"I thought I'd surprise you," she answered

looking around. "I brought donuts for you and Ross. Where is he?"

Virginia moved further into the kitchen wondering if she might find Tristan's assistant hiding behind one of the appliances.

"He broke his leg while we were working in the attic yesterday," Tristan said. "Went to the emergency room. The doctor says he won't be able to work for another few weeks. So...I'm on my own here until I can find someone else."

Virginia turned back to face him. For the first time, she realized just how tired he looked. There were shadows beneath his eyes, his light brown hair was rumpled and his face looked distinctly worried.

"But, you will find someone, right?" She asked feeling a mixture of pity for Tristan and concern for the project. After all, this was much more than a one-man job. Tristan would surely need help.

"I've been calling all night and this morning, every guy I know," he said. "They're all either busy on other projects, on summer vacation or out with injuries. So, it looks like, for now at least, I'm on my own. Though truthfully, I'm not sure how long I'll be able to keep it up once I get to the bigger stuff."

He moved over to the counter where Virginia had set down the donuts and leaned against it. He stared at the box but didn't seem to have strength left to even lift it open.

Virginia looked at him and felt an old tug in her heart. She'd felt it before, many times when she saw someone else in crisis. Her aunt told her it was her own special gift.

"God gave you a soft heart for other people," Aunt Emily use to say. "That's a strength, not a weakness. When God tugs on your heart and asks you to help someone, you should always listen to him."

Maybe it was the memory of her aunt's

voice in her head that made her do what she did next. Maybe she was simply bored with Jason being gone on his business trip and Samantha away at school all day and at work every night lately. Either way, she didn't think too long before saying to Tristan:

"Maybe I could help."

Tristan stopped staring at the unopened box and turned to look at Virginia, his eyes even wider than they had been when she'd stepped into the kitchen one moment before. She could see his mind racing between his initial instinct to say no, mixed with his absolute desperation for a solution to the situation.

"Virginia," he said hesitantly. "It'll be a lot of work and I wouldn't feel right taking up too much of your time."

Virginia gave him a smile and rolled her eyes.

"Tristan, if I've got time to take surprise

trips up here with homemade bakery items in hand, then I've clearly got time to help with the house renovations."

Tristan looked at her thoughtfully. His eyes traveled her body up and down as though trying to decide what type of work she would physically be able to do. Now, it was Virginia's turn to blush.

""Are you sure you want to do this?" Tristan asked.

"Absolutely," she answered confidently. "What do we need to do first?"

With one last skeptical glance, Tristan finally shrugged his shoulders and relented. "Well, what I really need is to tear down this wall right here. It takes two people."

"I take it that's why you were swearing at it when I came in," Virginia said with a grin. Tristan smiled as his cheeks turned flush once more.

"Well," she said, rolling up her sleeves and

moving past him to face the stubborn wall "Let's do it."

Tristan gave her a large hammer which she was surprised to find she could swing quite well after a couple of tries. Once they started, it was clear why Tristan had been cursing the kitchen wall. It was particularly stubborn. But, the longer she hammered at it, the easier it became. In fact, once she found a rhythm, it became easier and easier. Eventually, she realized she was enjoying herself. As she tore the wall down she felt a release, she felt strong, capable, she felt amazing! When they were done she turned to Tristan and exclaimed, "What can we tear down next?!"

"Whoa, slow down there tiger," he laughed. "Next we've gotta move out to the deck." He walked over to the counter where the unopened donut box still lay and flickered her a boyish, hopeful glance. "But I was wondering if maybe we could have a tiny snack break first...? I don't know what's in there, but the smell is so good, I think I'm addicted to it already." Virginia laughed and popped open the cardboard top. Tristan's mouth fell agape at the impressive looking pastries.

"Those look incredible. Where'd you get them?" he gushed, lifting a cream colored donut with chocolate glaze and a peanut butter crumble to his mouth.

"I make them," Virginia said feeling warmly proud. "Be warned, I'm trying out a new recipe on you."

Tristan nodded excessively while he gave her an emphatic thumbs up and chewed, rolling his eyes in obvious approval. Virginia had to laugh as she took a small bite out of her own. Two and a half donuts later, Tristan's vitality looked restored.

"I have no words for how amazing those are, but I'm pretty sure I could live on them if that gives you an idea." He grabbed up his hammer and gave a little yelp of enthusiasm. "Ready to get to it?" he exclaimed.

"Lead the way," Virginia chorused. She followed Tristan out to the deck with the kind of energy she hadn't felt in years. It seemed strange but, even though she could feel her muscles aching and the sweat running down her brow from the effort it had taken to knock down those walls, she didn't feel tired at all. In fact, she felt invigorated.

"We'll have to remove the rotted wood on the deck," Tristan said. "That means most of the railing will have to go. We'll start with that. Probably get to the lower boards tomorrow."

It turned out that taking the railing of the deck out was much more time consuming and not nearly as fun as tearing down walls. It was tedious work that required pulling the rusty nails from the boards up and out, before setting the rotting planks aside.

Luckily, as they worked, Tristan regaled her with amusing stories from some of the houses he had worked on before this one.

"I learned a lot from my dad," Tristan said. "He worked for a construction company and he used to do little projects around our house. The first time I broke my arm as a kid was when we were building a fort in the back yard."

"The first time?" Virginia asked pulling a nail up from a board.

"Definitely wasn't the last," Tristan answered. "After my third trip to the emergency room, my mom wanted to put an end to our weekend construction projects, but my dad wouldn't hear of it. 'If we keep the boy from falling down he'll never learn how to get back up'. That's what he always said."

"Can't say I blame your mom," Virginia said imagining what it would be like to take her own hypothetical child to the emergency room every other week. "It can't have been easy on her."

"Yeah, I realize that now," Tristan said. "Still, I'm glad my dad kept me working. If he didn't I wouldn't be doing what I'm doing now."

"You do seem to enjoy it," Virginia said. He turned and grinned at her, blue eyes glinting through a face full of sweat. Virginia had to admit that it looked good on him. The hard work, sweat and sheer physical effort. It was made more appealing by the fact that he truly did seem to enjoy it.

Even in the relatively hot afternoon sun, he never complained. In fact, the warmer and more difficult the work got, the more excited he became.

"I was thinking of replacing the wood out here with some local pine," he said eagerly surveying the outer edge of the now railless deck. "It would look better with the surroundings than the oak that's here now."

Virginia, who was not quite finished with the rails on her side gave a grunt of approval as she ripped a particularly stubborn nail from the oak finish. She was standing at an odd angle trying with all her might to budge the things, and when it finally came out, she felt herself falling forward. With a little scream, she landed face first on the forest floor beneath the deck; her forehead hit against something small but very hard. Something that felt like it was made of metal.

"Virginia!" she heard Tristan call out. His footsteps sounded on the deck rushing over to her. "Virginia, are you ok?"

She pushed herself up from the ground and was about to answer when the piece of metal that had hit her forehead, gleaming in the sun, caught her eye. She reached down slowly and, wiping the dirt off of it, picked it up.

"Virgina? Are you-"

"My key!" she said in surprise, barely hearing Tristan's voice on the deck above her.

"Your...your what?" he asked.

She grasped the little bronze key with an ornate handle similar to the house key, in the palm of her hand and pushed herself up.

"I buried it years ago," Virginia said turning to Tristan, "So my sister wouldn't find it."

He reached down and offered her a hand up, still looking perplexed. She grasped his hand and allowed him to pull her up to the porch, the other hand still clutching the cool bronze.

"Is it a key to the house?" Tristan asked. "Why wouldn't you want your sister to find that?"

"No," Virginia said with a little chuckle as she opened her palm and showed the key to him. It was much, much smaller than a house key. Smaller even than a mail key. "It was the key to my diary."

"You had a key for your diary?" Tristan asked. He still looked confused, but amused at the same time, as though he thought it might be some kind of joke.

"Lots of girls have locks for their diaries," Virginia said. "That way no one can see what we write about."

"And what kind of stuff did you write about?" Tristan asked. She looked him in the eye and he immediately shifted his gaze away from her, his cheeks turning that embarrassed pink color. "I mean, I'm just curious. I didn't have any sisters or anything so, I don't really know about that kind of stuff."

He looked so adorably awkward that she just had to laugh before answering.

"That's ok," she said. "It's not a big secret or anything. Mostly I just wrote about things that were going on in my life. Really, if anyone had read it they would have been bored to tears. Though, I guess I did write about boys sometimes."

"Boys?" Tristan asked.

"Of course!" Virginia said. "I was twelve. Almost thirteen. That's what girls that age start to think about. Isn't that true for boys too?"

Tristan shrugged, obviously more intrigued now than embarrassed.

"I guess," he said, "but we certainly didn't write about it in diaries."

"No," Virginia said with a teasing smile. "You probably just kept it all bottled up inside until it exploded in a fit of unexpected rage."

"What can I say?" Tristan said jokingly. "That's the manly way."

There was only a bit more work left to do on the deck. Once they were finished, the sun was starting to hang low in the sky. Virginia knew that the last ferry of the day would be making its way towards the dock any minute.

"I'd better start heading out," she said. "I don't want to miss the last boat."

"I'll drive you," Tristan said, gathering his tools. "The dock's on the way to my apartment anyway."

"Thanks," Virginia said. As they climbed into Tristan's small blue truck, she began to realize just how little she actually knew about him.

Despite the stories he'd told her about his dad as they worked, he offered no specifics. He didn't tell her where the house with the tree fort was located. She didn't know if he'd grown up in Sweetwater or in Seattle or even in the state of Washington. And, now, as she watched him drive through the small downtown and make his way to the ferry, she couldn't help but feel an intense curiosity about this man beside her.

"So," she began as they passed the old ice

cream parlor, feeling a bit awkward. "I guess you grew up on the island."

"No, actually," he answered. "I grew up in Northern California. A little town called Thousand Oaks."

"Oh," she answered turning to him now more than curious. She'd assumed that he was a local boy. "How did you find yourself here then?"

His face suddenly fell and she saw his lips purse closed. There seemed a longer than normal pause before he answered.

"I...um...well, I graduated high school and a buddy of mine was planning to move to Seattle. Asked if I wanted to join him. I said yes," he answered.

"So, that's how you got to Washington," she said, "but what made you move all the way out to the island?"

Now his cheeks turned red, but it wasn't with the kind of adorable embarrassment she'd seen earlier. This looked a lot more like shame.

"I just...I guess I just wanted a change," he said.

She knew immediately that it wasn't the full story. Still, she also knew that it was best not to press. After all, she was his employer. Plenty of employers didn't know their employee's life stories. And that was fine. In fact, it was often better that way. They drove in silence for several more minutes until they arrived at the dock just as the last ferry was pulling up, packed with rush-hour passengers commuting home to the island from the city.

"Thanks for helping out today," he said. "I really appreciate it."

"No problem. It was fun," she answered genuinely. "Will you need someone to help out tomorrow?"

He looked at her, his eyes wide and blinking in surprise.

"You...you want to help out tomorrow too?" he asked.

"Yeah," she answered. "I haven't got anything else to do. Besides, like you said. It's a two-man job."

"Oh. Ok," he said slowly as though still trying to process what she was saying. "Could...could you be here by nine?"

"Absolutely," Virginia said.

"Ok then," he answered with an impressed smile. "I'll see you tomorrow."

They said goodbye and Virginia made her way onto the ferry, walking much more quickly than she had getting off.

She hadn't felt this good about her day in years. Maybe it was that she spent the entire day being productive. Maybe she just needed more exercise like the kind she got when she worked on the house.

No matter the reason, as she stood on the deck watching the sun sink lower into the sky over the bay, Virginia couldn't help the consuming smile that crept across her face.

Chapter 7.

Virginia ended up going out to Sweetwater almost every weekday she could for the next several months. Each time, she found herself parking her car at the bay and taking the ferry over as a foot passenger.

She found that she enjoyed the walk through the woods and up to the cottage much more than she did the drive. Even if the drive did take her through the quaint downtown, the woods gave her space and time to think. It made her concede that her sister was right about Virginia's preference for country over city life.

She was starting to realize that she felt more at home among the hills and pine trees of Sweetwater than she did amidst the concrete, traffic and noise of Seattle. Beyond that, her appearance had even begun to show improvement.

Three weeks after she'd started working on the renovations with Tristan, she noticed that she'd lost a bit of weight. The sun had given her pale skin a tan and put the healthy glow that she'd had when she was younger back into her cheeks.

Even Jason had noticed a difference.

"I see you've finally started on that diet," he'd quipped one night at dinner, "It's paying off."

"Thanks," Virginia said, "but I've been eating normally. Just been walking a lot. And working on the house has really helped."

He'd paused at that and looked down at his plate. For a moment, Virginia thought that she'd said something wrong, or that he wasn't all that pleased to hear her mention her work on the island.

A moment later, however, he looked back at her with that same charming smile that was so familiar.

"I've always said you should exercise more," he said. "I mean, that's how I've stayed in such good shape."

He set down his fork and pulled up the sleeve of his shirt. Virginia had to stop herself from rolling her eyes when she realized what he was going to do.

Sure enough, with a chuckle, he flexed his still very firm bicep.

"See? Just look at that," he said.

"I know," Virginia answered with a smile, trying to hide her weariness. "Solid as a rock."

"Solid as a rock," she repeated. They didn't mention the island or the house the rest of the night.

Yet Jason's indifference, for a reason Virginia could not explain, seemed to spur on her trips to Sweetwater. She almost felt as though she were doing something rebellious by going to help Tristan every day. Which, of course, she wasn't. She and Tristan didn't do anything other than work on the house while she was there. Of course, he did occasionally drive her back to the ferry. And now that many of the primary renovations were nearly completed, they had gone into town together to look at furniture a few times. But that was only because there was no one else to furniture shop with. Sam had no desire to visit the island and Jason always claimed he was much too busy with work to come with her. This was something that even Tristan took note of as they walked through the antique shop looking at several wooden wardrobes that might fit into the master suite.

"You know," he said. "I just realized I've yet to meet this famous boyfriend of yours."

"Jason's an account executive for a television station," Virginia answered running her hand down the front of a handsome set of drawers made of chestnut. "They keep him pretty busy there."

"Hmm," Tristan said. Though, Virginia was certain there was something behind his vocalization. She turned from the chestnut set of drawers to her companion.

"What does that mean?" she asked, noticing too late how defensive her voice sounded.

"Nothing," Tristan said though he didn't look at her. Instead, he turned his gaze to a nice pinewood desk beside an old bookshelf.

"Just...if my girlfriend was working on a house that meant this much to her...I don't know. I'd at least want to come and see it once or twice."

Virginia, not sure at all how to answer that, turned back to her wardrobe.

They didn't speak for several moments, both pretending to examine their own individual artifacts. Though Virginia had a feeling that Tristan was about as focused on his desk as she was on the wardrobe in front of her.

"You know, I've been wondering," Tristan said finally turning to her. "Whatever happened to the diary? You know, the one the key belonged to?"

"Oh, I think I threw it away," Virginia said. Glad that the subject of Jason had apparently been dropped. "See, after I buried the key, I forgot where I put it. And, a diary without a lock is pretty useless. So, I stopped using it. Eventually, I think I must have gotten rid of it."

"You just...got rid of your innermost thoughts?" Tristan said turning from his desk to look at her as though she were insane. "Do most girls do that with their diaries?"

"I don't know, to tell you the truth," Virginia said. "Some keep them, I guess. But, like I said, my teenage thoughts were not exactly noteworthy. Mostly it was stuff about the weather, crushes, which were probably on tv characters, some early sketches."

"Sketches?" he asked interestedly. "Like drawings?"

"Yeah," she answered. "I've always liked painting and drawing. I even got my major in art history in school. I really started sketching up here during the summers."

"So, you're an artist," he said. "And here I thought you were just a trust fund kid with a penchant for baking."

With a laugh, she reached over and swatted him playfully on the arm. He side stepped away from it with a chuckle of his own.

"You know I teach art at the elementary schools," she said.

"Well, yeah," he said. "But, anybody could do that. I didn't know that you really drew stuff."

Virginia rolled her eyes at him. The idea that anybody could teach art, even to young children, was an idea she'd been fighting against since she took up her career.

"Why'd you stop?" Tristan asked.

"Who says I stopped?" Virginia said, not looking at him. She felt heat race through her features when she realized that Tristan had come closer to the truth than even she realized.

"You never talk about painting," he said. "Or drawing. You talk about baking, about your boyfriend, about your aunt and your sister. But, you never talk about art."

She went silent for a moment as she found

herself fiddling with the handle of the wardrobe. Not for any particular reason, just to give her hands something to do while she tried her best to think of a way to answer him.

"Well, I...I mean...I did think about going to graduate school," she said. "Getting a master's degree. I even wanted to teach college at one point, but then Jason decided to go to graduate school and I had to get a job to help him out."

"But, he's got a job now, doesn't he?" Tristan asked. "Have you thought about going back to school now."

Virginia, still unsure what to say, simply shrugged.

"I don't know," she answered as honestly as she could. "Maybe when the house is finished. Then at least I'll have some time to think about it."

There was a moment of silence. Eventually, Virginia dared to look from the wardrobe handle back up to Tristan. He was staring at her, blue eyes narrowed and focused. It reminded her vaguely of the way Samantha looked at her when she knew Virginia was hiding something. Maybe it was the sudden resemblance between them that made Virginia slightly unsettled.

Finally, the look disappeared from Tristan's face and he smiled at her.

"Well, I'm happy to keep you busy until then," he said.

"I'm happy to be busy," Virginia answered. "There are only so many donuts I can bake, after all."

They decided that they would buy the chestnut wardrobe for the master suite. Virginia also bought a few odds and ends that she would put in the bedroom. It was mostly antique doll furniture, the kind she'd loved when she was a little girl. The kind her aunt definitely would have approved of being in her home.

Tristan arranged for the wardrobe to be delivered to the house the next day and Virginia took her purchases with her in two bags.

"Do you want me to keep that stuff in the truck?" Tristan asked. They would be driving right from the antique store to the ferry at the dock. While the packages were not particularly heavy, they were awkwardly wrapped.

"No," Virginia answered feeling determined. "I want my sister to see the doll furniture set I got. I know she'll love it. It's just like the one we used to have when we were little."

"As long as you're sure it'll be ok," Tristan said looking skeptically as she tried to maneuver the packages into the truck cab in a way that would leave room for her to sit. No matter how she tried, the unwieldy bags did not seem to want to make room for her.

Finally, she gave up and agreed to put them in the bed of the truck. Tristan popped that tailgate down and gave Virginia a hand as she climbed into the back of the pickup. He handed her up the bags, then stood back and watched. Virginia took the two bungee cords Tristan had and criss-crossed them over the packages, securing them to the truck tie down hooks. Tristan stood with his arms crossed, watching with an inner amusement as she scurried back and forth, locking her goods in place. When she was satisfied that they wouldn't blow away once they started driving, Virginia stood up, proudly placed her hands on her hips and proclaimed, "We are good to go!"

She made her way to the back of the cab, but before Tristan could move to help her down, she hopped off the back of the tailgate and down to the ground. As Virginia's feet landed on the loose, rocky asphalt, her shoe caught on the gravel and sent her flying forward. Tristan could do barely more than open his arms to catch her. Luckily, he was quick enough and grabbed her just before she hit the ground. His arms flung around and secured her tightly. Virginia quickly scrambled to regain her footing, gripping Tristan's strong shoulders to pull herself up. She tried to hide her embarrassment as she stood to thank him. As soon as she was upright, her breath caught immediately in her chest. He was much closer than she'd anticipated and his eyes were once again, giving her that penetrating, searching look. Only this time, they didn't remind her of her sister's at all. Virginia blinked then forced a chuckle.

"Thanks," she said lowly while straightening up and moving slightly away from him.

Tristan re-opened her car door and helped her in. She tried to busy herself so as not to watch him walk around to get in on the other side. They didn't speak on the short drive back up to the ferry, but the entire way there Virginia felt that tug in her chest. She knew this was the same one her Aunt Emily had told her to listen to.

She didn't know what it was saying, exactly. And even if she did guess, she thought, she wasn't sure that she should listen to it this time.

As she said goodbye to Tristan, took her packages and made her way onto the ferry, the tug in her chest grew stronger. And strangely, so did the memory of Tristan's secure arms wrapped around her.

Chapter 8.

"You're coming on the camping trip, right? None of your bags look packed yet."

Virginia turned from the skillet where the tofu stirfry for dinner was cooking to look at her sister. Samantha was leaning against the kitchen counter, purse in hand, ready to head out the front door as soon as Jason showed up.

"I don't know," Virginia said turning back to the stovetop. "Tristan might need me on the island. We've still got a decent amount of work to do on the house to finish it up."

"Turning down the annual cousins camping trip to do manual labor?" Samantha said a teasing note of surprise in her voice. "Either you really like this contractor guy or you're thinking about going into the construction business."

Virginia turned to Samantha over her shoulder and gave her sister a half-hearted glare. Sam had been teasing Virginia about Tristan for the past week, ever since Virginia had shown her the doll furniture and told her how Tristan had helped to pick it out.

"You know I've always liked interior decorating," Virginia said. "And, who knows, maybe I will start up another side business."

"I'd have thought you were too busy for that," Sam said. "Between baking and your job during the school year."

"I'm free during the summer, though," Virginia said. "And I only sell a few dozen donuts a month. It's not like I've got to be baking constantly to fill the orders."

She turned back to peer at her sister just in time to hear Samantha let out a scoff.

"Still," Sam said. "You never miss the camping trip. Not even when you do have donut orders to fill. You can try to hide it all you want, but there's something different going on at that house."

Virginia couldn't help but smile when she thought about that and she realized she didn't have any argument against it. It was true that being back at her Aunt's house, working so hard on it, seemed to have sparked something in her. She was much more cheerful now that she was busy arranging the rooms for showing and helping Tristan fix up the attic.

"It is coming along nicely," Virginia said. "In fact, now that we've got some of the furniture in, it looks better than it did when Aunt Emily was living there."

"Well, Aunt Emily had it cluttered with little doilies and stuffed animals," Samantha said. "I'm sure you've got a better eye than that."

Virginia rolled her eyes to herself again. It was true that Aunt Emily had a tendency to collect what most people would call clutter. And it was true that Virginia, while keeping the original aesthetic, had done away with some of the frills and Victorian dolls that her Aunt had been fond of. But she still liked Aunt Emily's taste. She'd always been more fond of it than her sister.

"And, I'm sure your contractor friend is helping a lot too," Samantha said slyly. Virginia felt another blush come into her cheeks. This was the most annoying thing about Samantha's teasing. Her sly implications about Virginia and Tristan.

What was worse, Virginia was never quite sure how to answer them. Of course she'd told

Samantha they were just good friends, which was the absolute truth, but every time Virginia made the assertion, it sounded fake. Hollow even to her own ears. She and Tristan had truly bonded as friends, as really good friends.

Finally, Virginia settled on an answer that might put both Samantha's teasing as well as her own strange fears to rest.

"You should come by one weekend and check the house out," Virginia said. "It's been awhile since you've been to the island. It's also been awhile since you've had a date. And Tristan is cute. Not to mention single."

Sam scoffed as Virginia took the stirfry off the heat and allowed it to cool.

"Have you ever known me to be attracted to the handyman type?" Sam asked. Virginia had to admit that Samantha had a point about that. Despite her derision of Jason as "pretty boy", Samantha had always been attracted to men of Jason's type. Clean cut city boys who had rarely if ever done any actual work with their hands.

"Besides, I wouldn't want to take him away from my big sister," Sam said with another teasing smile. Virginia cursed herself silently when she felt her cheeks begin to grow warm again. She took a breath and made a vain attempt to laugh it off.

"That's not a great thing to joke about with a girl who's about to get engaged," Virginia said.

Sam rolled her eyes.

"Has pretty boy put a ring on your finger yet?" She asked.

"Not yet," Virginia admitted. "But, when the house is sold he-"

"Do you know that? For sure?" Sam asked. She was giving Virginia that pointed look. The one where she narrowed her eyes and tried to look through her.

Virginia tried to think of some argument, a

definitive come back she could make, but realized that she had none. The truth was, she couldn't be absolutely sure that Jason would propose once the house was sold. They'd talked about it as if it were a fact for the last few years, but, nothing seemed definite.

Still, Virginia knew she had to come up with some answer. She opened her mouth, hoping that something would come to her. Luckily, at that moment, the doorbell rang.

Silently thanking Jason's timing, she moved to the front door while her sister followed, purse in hand, ready for work.

"Hey babe," Jason said when she opened the door. She was slightly embarrassed, but not shocked to see that he had, once again brought his own six-pack.

"Hi Jason," Virginia said pulling him inside and giving him a quick peck on the lips.

"Hey Sam," Jason said pulling away from Virginia at seeing her sister behind her.

"What's up?"

Samantha didn't answer. She simply glared at him for a moment before pushing past him to the front door.

"Let me know if you're coming on the camping trip," Samantha said to Virginia over her shoulder as she made her way down the driveway.

"That's right," Jason said as Virginia closed the door behind her sister. "That camping trip with your cousins is this weekend, right?"

"Yeah," Virginia answered, leading Jason to the kitchen. Every year she, Samantha and two of their cousins from her dad's side got together at a state park for a girls camping trip. These were always a lot of fun and Virginia had never missed one before, which was why she felt slightly guilty about the desire to skip this year.

"It's good timing," Jason said sitting down

at the table and waiting to be served. "I'm going on another business trip to Portland."

"I thought you just went there a couple weeks ago," Virginia said surprised.

"Yeah," Jason said, "but the client wanted more time to think about the deal. So, a group of us have to go back this weekend. But if you're on that girls camping trip, I won't feel too guilty about leaving you alone again."

Virginia turned and offered him a weak smile as she moved to the table with both their plates in hand. She thought about not telling him her plans to go to the cottage instead. After all, if he was going to be gone, he wouldn't really care where she was. And there was no chance of Samantha telling him. She never gave Jason the time of day anyway.

Her conscience grappled over the idea for a minute, then decided that felt that too much like a kind of betrayal. She'd always prided herself on being completely honest with Jason and she was determined that wouldn't stop now.

Taking a deep breath as she sat down to her dinner, she told him the truth.

"Actually," Virginia said. "I'm not sure if I'm going to go on the camping trip this weekend."

"What do you mean?" Jason asked, taking a bite of tofu. "You go every year."

"Well...yeah," Virginia said, "but we've still got some work to do on the house. I'm doing the interior decorating now and I don't want to leave Tristan there all weekend with a whole bunch of work still to do."

The casual smile on his face faded at the mention of Tristan. His expression seemed to darken as he put his fork down on his plate.

"You've been spending a lot of time up there already, haven't you?" he asked.

"Well, as I've said, since Ross, Tristan's assistant got hurt, I've kind of stepped up to fill in," she said. "We've done a good job all things considered. We should have it done within the next couple weeks or so."

"And you really think spending the weekend there is going to speed things up?" he asked skeptically. Virginia looked across the table and gave him a reassuring smile.

"I won't be spending the weekend there," Virginia said. "Just Saturday during the day. I'd be back here with the last ferry."

His skeptical expression didn't change. His hazel eyes met hers and they were darker than Virginia had ever seen them. For the first time, they didn't dance or pierce her heart, there was something sulky and almost jealous in them.

"I was actually going to ask you to come up and see it this weekend," Virginia said hurriedly. It was true, she had thought about asking Jason to come up with her to look at the house. He hadn't seen it at all since they'd started doing renovations.

"But I didn't realize you had a work trip," Virginia said.

"I can't get out of it," Jason snapped, a peevish note in his voice.

"I know that," Virginia said, "I didn't ask you to. You can come up some other weekend maybe. Or once we're finished."

With slight hesitation, she glanced back up at him. That dark expression was still there. For some reason, it made Virginia shiver unpleasantly.

"I still think he's making you do too much work," Jason said finally pulling his eyes back to his plate. "You're paying him, remember? Not the other way around."

"I like doing it," Virginia said, though she noticed her voice was smaller than she'd meant for it to be. "Besides, like I said, we're almost done."

"Well I'm glad of that," Jason said. He

didn't look at her but stabbed his food a little more forcefully than was necessary.

Virginia watched her boyfriend the rest of the night, noting what a strange mood talk of the house seemed to put him in. If she didn't know better, she would have guessed that Jason was jealous. Jealous of the time she was spending with the house, and with Tristan.

That was surprising, to say the least. Jason had always been self-assured, brimming with confidence. This new side of him was surly and possessive and she wasn't at all sure that she liked it.

Even though they didn't mention the house or the island again, she felt that same surly attitude from him the rest of the evening. No matter what she did or said, she couldn't seem to shake him from it.

When he went home that night, for the first time since they'd been together, she was glad to see him go.

Chapter 9.

On Friday night, Virginia told her sister that she wouldn't be coming on the camping trip. Samantha, to Virginia's surprise, was not at all upset by her sister's announcement.

"Say hi to your friend for me," Sam said with a wink as she left the house on Saturday morning. Virginia rolled her eyes as her sister closed the door, but felt her cheeks grow warm.

As soon as Sam left, she packed up another

batch of donuts she'd baked to share with Tristan for breakfast and headed to the ferry.

It was only a little past nine in the morning when she arrived on the island. The normally warm August sun was still fairly low in the sky, its power not as strong as it would be in the afternoon. This, combined with the light mist that still hung along the wooded path to the cottage, made the walk quite pleasant. Virginia stopped several times to watch a hare cross the path in front of her as quickly as it could. She remembered naming the furry brown creatures when she was younger. She and her sister even developed ways to tell them apart, then named them accordingly.

When she arrived at the cottage, she moved quickly past the familiar sight of Tristan's truck parked out front and hurried inside.

Looking around the hallway, she couldn't help but smile at their handy work. The newly restored floor gleamed as the light from the front windows shined down onto it. The smell of sawdust had almost completely disappeared from the rooms around her. The walls in the family room had been expanded and the antique accent pieces gave the entire house a cozy feel.

This feeling was complimented by the dark, rich scent of coffee wafting from the kitchen. Virginia lifted her head and followed the scent, feeling a bit like a character in a cartoon led on to some mischief by the smell of apple pie.

When she moved into the kitchen, she found Tristan fiddling with an old fashioned coffee maker on the counter.

"I hope you made enough for everyone," she quipped. As usual, he jumped when she spoke before turning around and giving her a wide smile.

"Are those donuts?" he asked immediately.

"Well, they're not brussel sprouts," she said

moving to set the box on the kitchen counter. His smile widened and she nearly laughed as he rushed to the box.

"Virginia you are a lifesaver," he said opening the box eagerly and immediately stuffing a glazed donut into his mouth.

This time, Virginia let out a full laugh.

"You'd think you hadn't eaten in a week," Virginia said.

"I feel like I haven't," Tristan answered. "Spent most of last night working in the attic. I had to replace most of the wood before I could put in the insulation. Didn't get home until almost nine o'clock."

When she looked into his face, she could tell immediately that this was the truth. Though his smile was just as bright as normal, it was a bit weary and, once again, he looked slightly worse for wear.

"Did you get it finished?" Virginia asked.

"Not quite," he said. "Honestly, I wouldn't

mind some help in there this morning."

Virginia, who had learned early on not to be picky about the tasks she was handed in this project, none the less, put on a teasing skeptical smirk.

"Is this the same attic where your last assistant broke his leg?" she asked.

"That depends," he said swallowing a bit of donut and leaning towards her across the counter. "Are you scared to go up there?"

Virginia looked into his eyes and felt another little tug in her heart. They were not close together. Definitely not as close as they had been the night he'd kept her from falling on her face in his truck. Even so, that same tug was there. It made her feel strange and more than a little uncomfortable.

Finally, she gave a nervous laugh and backed away from him.

"I've been up there plenty of times," Virginia said. "Nothing about this house scares me anymore. But, if I do break my leg, it's coming out of your check."

Tristan let out a laugh as well and Virginia thought it sounded almost as nervous as her own.

"Fair enough," he said.

After two cups of coffee and several donuts; they headed up to the attic. She couldn't help but marvel at the thought that Tristan had eaten almost half the box by himself. As it turned out, Tristan had done a good bit of the insulation the night before. The rest took the two of them no more than a couple of hours. By lunch time, they were back in the kitchen eating two decent corned beef sandwiches that Tristan had packed.

"So, what needs doing after lunch?" Virginia asked.

"Well," Tristan said taking a sip from his bottle of water which he'd also brought in his lunch sack. "The only thing we've really got left to do are the two small bedrooms. And that's not going to require any real manual work. It's just going through the old stuff in there, deciding what you want to keep, and what needs to ne boxed up."

"Sounds right up my alley," Virginia said. Feeling a tiny thrill of excitement. Ever since they started this project, she'd been waiting to go back into her old bedroom. She couldn't help but feel curious about how many of her old childhood treasures Aunt Emily had decided to keep.

She soon discovered that there was more in her old bedroom than she ever could have imagined. Almost everything she remembered from her childhood was stacked in boxes inside the closet whose door was falling off its hinges.

"I'll fix the closet if you promise to sort through the boxes," Tristan said. Virginia was more than happy to agree.

This task took a lot longer than either of them had expected. Each box brought on a flood of new memories. Virginia would come to a sudden stop and exclaim excitedly each time she came across another little treasure.

"Oh! My jewelry box!" she said pulling out a handsome brown chestnut box that had been a present from her Aunt Emily when she was only eight years old. "My old bracelets are still in here!"

She happily moved through a pile of clunky costume bracelets. Most of them in lavishly bright colors. Suddenly, she had an idea.

"You know, I think I finally know where that key's going to go," she said fishing the small diary key that she'd taken to keeping in her pocket.

"You're going to put the key in the jewelry box even though the diary's been thrown away?" Tristan asked with a small chuckle.

"It's a memory," Virginia said with a shrug. "And, since I can't read my diary any more, this is all I've got left of it. I might as well keep it.

"The last memory of all your innermost thoughts as a teenage girl?" Tristan asked as he watched Virginia set the key amidst her bracelets and close the jewelry box lid.

"Something like that," she said.

"You're lucky, you know," he said. "My parents threw all this kind of stuff out when I moved away."

"Why would they do that?" Virginia asked curiously. She knew that both her aunt and her mother had held on fervently to Virginia and Samantha's childhood toys. They didn't go in the trash bin until Sam and Virginia said they should.

When she looked at Tristan, his face sunk slightly.

"Well, it was my dad, mostly," he said.

"See...he and I didn't part on great terms. He wanted me to stay and go into his business. I wanted to work on my own. He still hasn't really forgiven me, I don't think."

Virginia saw Tristan's lips purse closed and his eyes dart to the side. It was apparent that this was a subject he wasn't particularly keen on. Virginia couldn't blame him, she knew fighting with your parents was always painful.

Instead of answering, she grabbed hold of another box.

"Oh my gosh! I'd forgotten about this," she said when she saw what was written in black sharpie on the side of the brown cardboard.

"What is it?" Tristan asked, thankful for a change in subject.

"Virginia Ellis Originals," she read from the side of the box. "It's what my aunt called my paintings. She said they were going to be worth a lot of money one day."

Carefully, she opened the box and another

altogether different tug pulled at her heart when she saw the painting beneath the lid.

It was a landscape, detailing the view of the woods from the deck, there was even a hint of greenish blue, indicating the ocean beyond the trees. Virginia remembered sitting out on the deck for weeks one summer, carefully working on detailing the leaves of the trees, the color of the sky. She could even see the original, bright wood of the deck, just as it was in its prime.

"Can I see?" Tristan asked. Virginia looked up at him startled. She'd been so lost in the memory that she had nearly forgotten anyone else was in the room. Shaking herself awake, she passed the framed picture over to Tristan.

He took it gently and looked down at it. His eyes broadened and he tilted his head curiously. He took his hand and moved it over the frame as though he was trying to memorize it.

"This is...this is really good!" he said surprised.

"Thanks," Virginia said. "It's one of my first paintings. Not perfect, but I loved doing it."

"You can tell," he said. "The care definitely comes through."

He continued to look at it thoughtfully as though making some kind of decision.

"I think we should hang it in here," he said finally.

"What?" Virginia asked stunned.

"Why not?" Tristan asked. "We were going to need to buy some paintings for this room anyway. Why not hang one that's personal. That means something to the house."

Her first instinct was to say 'no'. She'd always been very cautious about who she showed her work to.

Then she remembered Aunt Emily. Her aunt had proudly displayed her nieces work not only in the bedrooms but also in the family and living rooms. Often despite Virginia's protests. If she wanted this house to be a tribute to her Aunt's memory, she had to admit that this was part of it. Besides, it was only for show. The pictures would come down when the new owners moved in.

"I...I guess we could," she said. "It'll save us money on art anyway."

They spent the rest of the afternoon hanging pictures. Tristan, like her aunt, insisted that Virginia's prints be hung not only in the bedrooms, but several other rooms as well. In the end, Virginia had to admit they added some personality to the place. Plus, they were specific to Sweetwater and the time she spent here; they meant something.

Tristan and Virginia worked hanging the pictures and sorting through boxes well into the late afternoon. By the time the last box was packed away in the newly insulated attic,

Virginia had completely lost track of time. It took Tristan, or rather Tristan's appetite, to remind her.

"We should probably get something for dinner soon," he said. "There's a Chinese take out place not far away."

The mention of dinner made Virginia pause as she walked down the stairs from the attic.

"Dinner? What time is it?" she asked.

"It's almost six," Tristan said.

Virginia's eyes widened and her heart began to pound. The ferry. She'd missed the ferry.

"I...I didn't plan on staying that long!" She said. "The ferry..."

"What?" Tristan asked. "The last one doesn't leave until seven, right?"

"On weekdays," Virginia reminded him. "The last one is at five thirty on Saturdays."

His face fell as he realized her predicament.

"Well...I mean I know it's a ways but...I've

got the truck. I could drive you back."

Virginia shook her head.

"They're doing construction on the bridge tonight," she said. "I saw the notice this morning on the ferry coming over."

Tristan furrowed his brow in thought, even as Virginia began to panic. As she ran through her list of options, the reality set in that there was no way she was getting off the island tonight.

Apparently, Tristan agreed with her internal assessment.

"How about this?" Tristan said thoughtfully. "I've got a buddy who runs a bed and breakfast in town. I'll call him and see if he can get you a room for tonight."

"Are you sure?" Virginia asked. "I...I wouldn't want to put anybody out."

"Don't worry about it," he said. "With that bridge, stuff like this happens all the time. Do you want me to give him a call?"

Though Virginia knew she didn't have much choice, she still hesitated. It was true that Jason was gone for the weekend and so was her sister. There was no real reason to go home, but she'd told Jason that she wasn't going to spend the night on the island.

No matter what else she did, she had always said that she would never break a promise, even an implied one, to her boyfriend. Still, now, there didn't seem to be any way to avoid it.

"Sure," Virginia answered in a slightly defeated tone.

She slumped down on the comfortable, worn in couch she had purchased for the living room, while she listened to Tristan talk to his buddy on the phone. It wasn't long before they appeared to have reached an agreement.

"Great, thanks man," Tristan said before

coming back into the room.

"Good news," he said. "My friend says he had someone cancel on him just this morning so, they've got a room open! They said you can head down to check in anytime before eight o'clock."

"Well then," she said, rallying her mood. "Sounds like there's time to order Chinese after all."

They ordered takeout and Virginia set up her iPad on the coffee table so that they could watch a movie on her Netflix account. As there was no WiFi set up at the cottage, she had to use her data but, she found she didn't care.

She picked a goofy comedy. The same kind that she used to watch with her aunt and sister during summers at the cottage. In fact, as she laughed out loud with Tristan on the couch, she couldn't help but think that, if they were eating frozen pizza instead of Chinese, she might as well have been back in her aunt's old living room watching VHS tapes on the little television screen.

The sun had begun to sink deeply down in the sky by the time the movie finished.

"You'd better start heading down the hill if you're going to make it to the bed and breakfast by eight," Tristan said. "I can drive you if you like."

"No thanks," Virginia answered feeling much more energetic than she'd felt that morning. "I think I'm in the mood to walk."

"In that case," Tristan said after a beat, "I'll walk with you."

"You don't have to do that," Virginia said with a small chuckle.

"I know I don't have to," Tristan answered. "But, I don't like the thought of you stranded in Sweetwater on your own. Besides, I could use a good walk."

Seeing no need and feeling no desire to argue anymore against his offer, Virginia accepted and the two of them headed down the hill towards town.

"Not many people out tonight," Virginia noted. "Saturday night, you'd think there'd be more activity. Even in a small town like this."

"It's actually more active on Friday night than Saturday," Tristan said. "A lot of people go to church on Sunday mornings here."

"I take it you do too," Virginia asked. "That's why you never work on Sundays I was assuming."

"I try to go pretty faithfully," Tristan said. "I thought Amanda may have mentioned it to you. She goes to the same church I do."

"She did say something about it," Virginia said. They walked along in silence for a good while. For some reason, the talk of church had sparked a guilty little twitch in her heart. It reminded her of the church her aunt used to take them to on Sunday mornings on the Island. It also reminded her how infrequently she went to church anymore in the city. She had one that she visited occasionally, maybe once every couple of months. It was nice, small and very traditional. When she went, she always felt as though she was the youngest person in the congregation. The fact that neither her sister nor her boyfriend was ever willing to go with her made the motivation to attend more difficult.

It suddenly struck her that while she was on the island, while working on her aunt's house, she had a feeling she owed it to Aunt Emily to go to a church service, for old time sake, if nothing else.

"So...what church do you go to?" Virginia asked. "Amanda never told me."

"Morning Star Bible," Tristan said. "It's a really small church. We actually meet in the old movie theater just two blocks from the bed and breakfast."

"Church in a movie theater?" she asked

raising an eyebrow. Tristan shrugged.

"The pastor didn't have enough money to build a new place and no one was using the theater," he said. "Besides, it seems to work well for us."

Virginia nodded and stared straight ahead as they walked. She felt strangely hesitant to ask Tristan what she knew she wanted to.

"So...what time does the service start tomorrow?" she asked finally.

He turned to her and even in the dying light of the sun she saw his eyebrows raise slightly.

"Do you...want to come?" he asked.

"Sure," Virginia answered. "I haven't been to church in awhile and I figure I should get back in the habit. That is...if it would be ok."

Tristan looked down, the corner of his lips twitching slightly in thought. He seemed just as hesitant to accept her offer to attend the church with him as she was to ask him if she could. Finally, she saw some kind of decision come into his eyes as he looked back over at her.

"Why not?" he said. "Service starts at ten. I'll come pick you up around nine thirty. We can walk over together."

"Sounds good," she said.

They reached the bed and breakfast which was tucked into a little house between two shops on the main street. An older, thin gentleman with gray hair greeted them.

"Frankly dear, I'm happy to have another guest," he said as Virginia signed in for her key. "If you hadn't come along it would be the third night in a row that room's gone unused."

As the owner left the the front desk to get Virginia's key from a hook in the back, she turned to Tristan.

"So, I guess I'll see you in the morning," she said. Even though she tried her best to make the farewell sound light and friendly, she couldn't help an odd shaking sound in her voice. She wasn't quite sure where it had come from.

"Yeah, see you then," Tristan said. For some odd reason, the shaking sound had come into his voice, too. He didn't move, but stood in the doorway looking at her oddly, as though he wanted to say something else, but wasn't sure if he should.

Finally, he seemed to decide against it. Instead of saying anything more, he simply gave her a tight-lipped smile and a nod before moving out the door.

Without thinking about it, Virginia moved to the window in the front lobby of the bed and breakfast and watched Tristan move down the street and back up the hill. The setting sun casting a long, dark golden shadow behind him as he moved.

Chapter 10.

As promised, Tristan met Virginia at the front of the bed and breakfast at nine thirty and they headed up the street together.

"I didn't have anything very nice," Virginia said reluctantly. "They let me use their washer and dryer last night for my jeans and t-shirt. But, I know it's not exactly church appropriate."

To her surprise, Tristan laughed.

"Trust me," he said. "It's perfectly

appropriate for this church."

When they reached the building, Virginia could see what he meant. Everyone there seemed to be in blue jeans and t-shirts. Some women were in dresses or skirts but, these were very much the minority.

People milled around the lobby of the movie theater talking and laughing as they sipped on free coffee from styrofoam cups or nibbled small donut holes. Everywhere Virginia looked, people seemed to be smiling and joking. It didn't remind her at all of the baptist church she'd been going to recently. It wasn't even like the old church her Aunt Emily used to take them to on Sundays.

In both the other places, church was a much more serious affair. Everyone dressed in their finest clothes and talked to each other in hushed tones as though laughter or loud speech might somehow offend God. There seemed to be no worry of that here.

"Uncle Tristan!" a small voice shouted from the other side of the lobby. Virginia turned to see a little girl in a pink shirt with a Disney princess on the front rushing towards Tristan with a determined look on her face.

Tristan let out a boisterous 'Hey!' as the little girl reached him. He leaned down, opened his arms and picked her up swinging her around once.

"Lilly!" he said. "It's so good to see you!"

"Lilly! There you are!" a voice very familiar to Virginia said. Sure enough, she turned to see Amanda striding towards them. A little boy no older than two years old on her hip.

"I'm sorry Tristan," she said. "But, Lilly's been wanting to see you for weeks. We haven't been able to get out to church for a while."

"Understandable," Tristan said. "I know it's a bit of a drive for you."

"Speaking of a bit of a drive," Amanda said turning to Virginia with a surprised, but pleased smile. "I'm amazed to see you here, Virginia. Especially this early."

"It's a long story," Virginia said wearily. "Suffice it to say, I ended up staying at a bed and breakfast here last night."

"She came to help with the house yesterday and we lost track of time," Tristan explained. Amanda laughed as the little boy on her hip began to poke at her cheek.

"Well, I can't say that hasn't happened to me," Amanda said. "Those ferry schedules can be chaotic."

Virginia was about to voice her agreement when a small voice at Tristan's feet stopped her.

"Why haven't you come to visit us?" Lilly asked looking up at Tristan with accusation lining her voice.

"I've wanted to," he said, "but I've been working on another house. It's really old, so it needs a lot of love."

"Doesn't our house need love too?" Lilly asked, unwilling to let the subject drop.

"I think your house has all the love it needs already," he said leaning down with a smile. "Remember, you've got to spread love around if you want it to do any good. And my friend Virginia's house needs just as much love as your house did."

Virginia smiled down at Lilly who looked skeptically up at this new competitor for her Uncle Tristan's time and attention.

It seemed whatever Tristan said about needing to spread his house-love-work time around, Lilly wasn't entirely buying it.

A moment later, they were all called into the theater for the service.

The service, like the lobby, was unlike anything Virginia had ever seen at a church. Before anything else happened, a band got up on the stage, which had an acoustic guitar and drum set already set up. Immediately, they began to play an upbeat tune that talked about how they could 'sing unending songs because of God's great love'.

All around her, people were clapping and singing. A few kids only a little older than Lilly even ran out into the aisles and started dancing, complete with well-practiced hand motions.

The mood was infectious. Soon Virginia found herself smiling and clapping along to the music. By the second song, she'd started to sing using the words projected onto the huge film screen behind the band.

When things slowed down on the third or fourth song, she realized that she was singing with her eyes closed and her hands raised. That tug in her heart was back and it was stronger than it had ever been before. Almost as firm as it had been the day in her Aunt's little church when Virginia had walked up the aisle and asked to be baptized.

It seemed as though the band stopped playing much too soon for Virginia's liking. She sat down in a seat next to Tristan as a man with a polo shirt, glasses and neatly cropped brown hair walked onto the stage. This, according to Tristan who leaned over and whispered in her ear, was the pastor.

The theme of the sermon, which was projected brightly behind the man on the big screen, was Change.

"Change is scary," the man affirmed. "God knows that. God knows a lot of times we don't want to change. He knows how comfortable we are in our own routine, our own lives. Even if our lives aren't perfect. Even if they're miserable, he knows that we won't want to change. Take, for example, the Israelites. They were slaves in Egypt. Forced into unpaid labor. Poor housing, little food, no freedom. But, when God takes them out of captivity, when God sets them free, are they happy?" he paused here and Virginia shifted uncomfortably in her seat. She shifted uncomfortably because she thought she knew the answer to that question. And, what's more, she thought she knew how it might apply to her.

"They were happy for a while," he said. "But as soon as things got a little bit difficult, what did they want to do? They wanted to go back. They wanted to go back to the way things were. Back to the world they knew. Back where, even if they weren't happy, they were comfortable." Virginia's discomfort grew as the pulsation in her heart began again. This time, Virginia knew, it would continue to grow much stronger than she'd ever felt it before.

"It would be easy for us to judge them, wouldn't it?" The pastor said. "It would be easy if we weren't exactly the same way. Think about it. Don't we all do the same thing? I know I do. Even when I know something's not good for me. Something doesn't make me happy. Something is pulling me away from my relationship with God or my family, I still don't want to give it up. Sometimes it's a pastime that's taken over. Sometimes it's spending too much time at work, hoping to earn that extra buck. Sometimes it's a relationship with someone and you just know is toxic. It's hurting both you and them but, you just don't want to let go of it. It's too comfortable."

Just as Virginia had predicted, the tug in her heart grew much more forceful. She thought about Jason and the urge to run from the pastor's words began to collide with that tug in her heart that insisted she stay and listen.

'When you feel that tug in your heart,' Aunt Emily's voice whispered in her memory.

"That's God talking to you. The best thing you can do is listen to him."

So she stayed.

"I'm here to tell you today, that as hard as it may be to give up whatever it is you're clinging to, as hard as it may be to change, you have to let go," the pastor insisted. "You have to trust God, close your eyes and take that leap. Because, I promise, he wants to lead you to something a thousand times better than anything you have right now. He wants to lead you to a land flowing with milk and honey. But, he can only do that, if you'll let go of your comfort. Let go of whatever it is that's holding you back and agree to follow him."

The pastor spoke longer but Virginia's mind stayed fixed on that one last line. 'Let go of whatever it is that's holding you back and agree to follow him.' Deep down, she had a feeling that God was speaking directly to her. And, what's more, she knew he was trying to tell her about Jason. She knew her relationship with her boyfriend was far from perfect. She always thought if they just had a little more money, enough for him to get her a ring, to propose, then they would be fine. But she was beginning to realize now that a diamond ring wouldn't fix her problems any more than a little more money would.

The fact was, she and Jason were two very different people. She knew that having differences was something that in and of itself wasn't a bad thing. But when those differences were so fundamental, like his refusal to go to church with her, the ease with which she knew he sometimes lied to her, the deep down feeling that he didn't truly respect the person she was...she just didn't know if those things could be fixed by sheer love and determination.

By the time the service had ended, she'd made something of a decision. She would have to sit down and have a serious talk with Jason. Perhaps the first really honest talk they'd had in several years.

She was still contemplating how best to go about this when little Lilly's voice once again burst into her thoughts.

"Grandma, can Uncle Tristan come to the park with us?" Lilly asked eagerly as Amanda, her little brother Mikey, Tristan and Virginia made their way through the doors of the church.

"Honey, I'm sure Tristan already has lunch plans," Amanda said.

"We don't actually, do we Virginia?" he asked, looking over at her.

"Uh...no, I guess not," Virginia answered a bit at a loss as to what was going on.

"Would it be ok if Virginia came too?" Tristan asked Lilly. The little girl's smile faded a little bit as she looked from Tristan to Virginia. Lilly's wide brown eyes were still skeptical as she sized up Virginia, however after a moment, she gave a silent nod of assent.

"Ok!" Tristan said happily. "Let's go then!"

"Race me!" Lilly said as the group turned towards the park on the other side of the movie theater.

"Not too fast," Amanda reminded as Tristan moved up where Lilly was.

"Ok," he said. "Ready, set, go!"

Tristan and Lilly both took off running, though Virginia noticed that Tristan moved deliberately slow. She knew he was doing this to give his little-legged opponent a fighting chance to make it to the park first.

"Sorry about that," Amanda said moving Mikey from one hip to the other. "I know a picnic in the park probably wasn't your first idea for lunch."

"Actually, it sounds nice," Virginia said. "I

haven't had a picnic in years. In fact, I think the last one I had was on the island."

"Well, this'll just be sandwiches," Amanda said, "but the kids seem to like it. And we've got plenty for you and Tristan."

As it turned out there were egg salad, peanut butter and jelly, as well as roast beef sandwiches. Apparently, Amanda didn't mess around when it came to packing lunch. These were complimented by several bags of chips. Virginia had to admit that the sandwiches Amanda made were far superior to Tristan's, but she still gave him an A for effort.

After lunch, Lilly insisted that Tristan push her on the swing, a task that Tristan readily agreed to. Virginia spent the afternoon talking about the house with Amanda and occasionally accepting blades of grass as gifts from little Mikey who seemed intent upon pulling up every bit of lawn in the park.

"Oh! Thank you!" Virginia said as Mikey

put another long blade of grass in her hand. The two-year-old smiled at her before running off to get more treats.

"So the house is coming along well?" Amanda said.

"Yeah," Virginia answered. "Really well. We've even got some artwork on the walls to show it. The whole thing should be ready in another week or two."

"Perfect," Amanda said. "I've already got a few clients lined up to see it."

Virginia felt a dull thud in her chest when Amanda reaffirmed the interest other people had in the house. This one, she knew was a feeling of sadness and loss mixed with guilt. After everything she'd done with the house, all the work she'd put into it, she wasn't sure that she wanted it to go to some stranger. Someone who wouldn't truly appreciate what it meant.

After several more swings, Amanda told the kids that it was time to say goodbye.

Despite several protests from Lilly who nearly insisted that Uncle Tristan come back to their house for dinner, Amanda and the kids parted ways with Tristan and Virginia at the front of the park.

"Do you need to check out of the bed and breakfast or anything?" Tristan asked. "You could do that, then I'll come pick you up to take you back to the ferry in about an hour."

"I checked out this morning," Virginia said. "Besides, I don't really feel like being alone at the moment. After that church service and a picnic, I think I'm ready for another adventure."

She said this in a light tone with a smile. That's why she was surprised when Tristan's face fell and he looked away from her, down at the ground the way he always did when he was embarrassed.

"It's just...it's just I've got to do something this afternoon. It...it won't take long but, you probably wouldn't want to come."

"Try me," Virginia said. As though unable to help himself, a small smile crept across his face.

"Ok," he answered reluctantly.

He led the way back up the hill to where his truck was parked and opened the door for Virginia to get in. They were completely silent as they drove, a strange kind of tension filling the air. They truck made it's way through downtown, past the movie theater, the park, down a ways toward the opposite side of the island and finally turned into a small neighborhood.

The houses along this street were quaint and most were nicely kept. A few had peeling paint or ill-kept lawns, which were the only things that told Virginia this was not a wealthy neighborhood.

They stopped and parked across the street from a small house that was painted yellow with white gables, similar to the ones on her aunt's cottage.

Tristan kept his eyes fixed on the little house, his shoulders tense as though he was waiting for something. Virginia had the urge several times to ask him what it was. But his tension was so high that, in the end, she didn't dare. Instead, she turned to the house and watched it expectantly with him.

Finally, a small family came out. First to emerge was a boy around twelve or thirteen, followed by a girl who was nine or ten. An older woman with gray hair and an ankle-length red dress followed them. All three of them got into the van parked in their driveway and drove off down the street.

Tristan kept his eyes on it until it disappeared in the distance.

"Wait here," Tristan said. The sound of his voice made her jump. She realized that he hadn't spoken since they'd stepped into the truck.

She didn't answer but gave a nod of her head as she watched him close the door and walk across the street to the house.

He marched purposefully up to the mailbox, slipped something small and white inside of it before closing it again and making his way back to the truck.

"What was-"

"Nothing," he said. "Don't worry about it."

They started the truck again and made their way back down the little house-lined street. Virginia kept glancing at Tristan on their journey back towards the ferry. They were just as silent now as they had been on their trip to the mysterious house. Tristan's face was still set, his jaw still tense.

Virginia had never seen him look that way. Tristan was usually so casual and down to earth. He laughed and smiled easily and never took himself too seriously. But now, he looked as though he might just break.

She had to know why, even if he didn't want to tell her. If she didn't find out, the tension might just break her, too.

They stopped at the parking lot that led to the ferry entrance. It was still another forty-five minutes before the ferry arrived. When he stopped the car but didn't move to get out, she figured it was her best chance to get what she needed out of him.

"So, are you going to tell me what that was all about?" she asked.

"I told you not to worry about it," Tristan said. "It's a long story."

Virginia rolled her eyes and pointed to the clock on his dash.

"We're early," she said. "There's plenty of time for a long story."

He turned to her and looked her right in the eye. He searched her face and she could see a deep pain beneath it for the first time.

"You really want to know?" he asked.

"I really do."

Tristan looked at her with blue eyes narrowed. Finally, he let out a long sigh and looked straight ahead at the water in the bay.

"It started about eight years ago," he said. "I'd just graduated from high school. Just moved to Seattle. And I...had some problems then."

"What sort of problems?" Virginia asked.

"Drinking problems," Tristan said darkly, still looking determinedly out at the water.

"Anyway, some buddies of mine invited me out to this bar a little ways from the city. It wasn't on Sweetwater, but the island just next to it. I drove because I knew I'd be out late."

He paused and she saw his jaw clenching tightly. "It was the worst mistake I've ever made." When she looked down at the steering wheel of the truck, she could see his hands clutching it so hard that his knuckles nearly turned white.

"Anyway, I had a bunch of drinks with my friends and by the time I was ready to drive home I was pretty hammered. My memory of it is pretty hazy, but apparently I didn't want to drive, so my buddy took my keys and convinced me to sleep in the back of the car. But then at some point, he decided to drive us back to the city. It was really early in the morning," he went on. "Amazingly, he didn't run into a tree or a rock or anything, until we got to the bridge. And then..."

His voice began to waver.

"...I don't remember what happened. I just remember seeing some headlights coming towards us. Then everything goes black. Next thing I knew, I woke up in the hospital with some cuts, some broken bones, and a bad headache. Police were there. They said...they said I was under arrest for vehicular homicide."

He pried one hand off the steering wheel and ran it over his face which had gone from ashen to red.

"They...they said that we'd swerved into the wrong lane and the car we ran into...it was pushed off the bridge and she...she died. She was on her way to pick up her two grandkids for the weekend from their mother who lived on the island. A boy and a little girl."

This one point brought Virginia's mind back to what had just happened in that neighborhood. What she'd seen Tristan do.

"Was...were those....those kids..." she began, unsure how exactly to ask the question.

He nodded. Now, she could see tears running down his cheeks as he brought his other hand up from the steering wheel and furiously whipped them away.

"Do you mind if we walk for a little bit?" he asked without looking at her.

"Of course not," she said as lightly as she

could and pushed open her car door. She couldn't believe what she had just heard. So many thoughts swirled through her mind as they made their way down to the rocky coastline. They had shared so many stories over the course of their new friendship, but she had noticed a certain avoidance when it came to why he'd moved to the island, why he hadn't seemed to really date much, and a few other topics that he always managed to skirt. She realized now that this was a person who was consumed with a deep guilt and it was probably something that guided much of what he did. She was amazed that he allowed himself to do work that made him as happy as it did, because as she listened to him, she got the distinct feeling that he didn't believe he deserved to have true happiness.

Tristan walked with his hands shoved deep in his pockets, stooping into the whirling wind coming off the bay. Virginia followed behind him, navigating the rocky terrain. Finally, Tristan came to a large, flat rock and sat down, still keeping his gaze focused far, far away from reality. Virginia settled into a smooth dip in the rock where she was partially sheltered from the wind by Tristan's body next to hers.

"My friend and I had both been thrown from the car. Nobody could remember anything. They put John into an induced coma because of brain swelling, none of our other friends that we were with that night had seen us leave, and everyone was looking to me for answers. I hadn't thought I was driving, but honestly, I couldn't remember. We had been so out of it, when they questioned me, it just felt like anything was possible. And the fact that it was my car, the police assumed that I had been the driver. After a couple of days in the hospital, they had me on so many painkillers and I was being questioned constantly, I didn't know what to think. I became convinced that

I'd done it."

She saw his eyes clench shut, and his face tense as he fought back the pain of the memory.

"When John woke up, there was a lot more confusion, and they held us both until an investigation could be launched. I sat there, day in and day out realizing what we'd done. It didn't matter who was driving, another person had lost their life. And for what? So that we could forget our stupid worries for a few extra hours? So we could be home in time to sleep off our hangovers the next day? There was nothing that could have justified her dying and me living." He swallowed hard, resolute in his statement. "And it's so hard to drive out the what-ifs. If I hadn't gone out that night, if I hadn't been so young and naive, so stupid to take my car, so many small variations, better choices...she'd still be here."

Virginia sat silently beside him, listening

and watching him.

"Eventually the police investigation obtained some video from a street camera that showed John driving and me laying down in the back. I was released and he was arrested. It was awful, every part of it was completely awful. Her family..." he trailed off.

"So I put a check in their mailbox every month," he said thickly. "I've...I've never met them. I thought about it. Initially it was why I moved to the island, in fact. Afterwards, they had moved here and, I, I just didn't know where else to go. For whatever reason, no matter how much I argued with myself, it was the only thing that made sense to me. I thought...maybe I could see them. Ask forgiveness. But, every time I've tried, I just...something stops me and I can't..."

His voice broke off and Virginia knew he wouldn't be able to say anymore. She looked at him for a few moments almost unable to process everything he'd said. Tristan, her strong, funny and often wise friend was now staring vacantly at the rocks a few feet in front of him, looking broken.

She realized then that her problems seemed very small compared to his. Her issues with Jason, her guilt over the house, weddings and days when she felt sorry for herself, all paled in comparison to the pain and guilt this man next to her was feeling.

Instinctively, before she could stop herself, she reached over and threw her arms around him in a fierce hug. He paused a moment, as though unsure of what was happening. Then, slowly, she felt his arms move around her. Before long, he was sobbing against her shoulder and she placed her hand on his head, the way she remembered her mother doing when she was upset. It always made her feel safe, to be held tightly like that.

She didn't know how long it was before he

pulled back, taking deep shuddering breaths. She pulled back too. Though her instincts told her that she shouldn't.

"Thanks," he said. His voice still thick as he was wiped his eyes and was regaining his composure.

"You know, I...I usually don't tell people that, I mean, I never tell anyone," he said. "Last time I did was at an AA meeting. You were a lot nicer to me than they were."

He offered her a small watery smile.

"I'm sure that's not true," she said.

"Well, they didn't boo or hiss," he said. "But, I didn't get hugged or have my head stroked either."

"You can thank my mom for that," Virginia said with an equally awkward smile. "That's what she always did for me when I was upset."

"Well, she was a wise lady; it works," he said.

They sat quietly for a moment. The air around them was still tense, but it was a different kind than it had been before. The sound of the rolling waves became more present than it had been.

"You are forgiven, you know?" she said. She didn't know exactly where the words came from but she knew they were true.

"God's forgiven you," she continued when he looked at her slightly disbelieving. "You don't have to prove anything to him. You know that, right?"

He stared at her for a moment before nodding slightly.

"Yeah," he said. "Yeah, I know."

He gave a small smile that told her, no matter what he said, he couldn't quite believe her. She was about to say something else to him, something consoling or fervent but, before she could, she heard the familiar call of the ferry horn.

"You'd better get going," he said with another weak smile. "Don't want to miss this one."

"Yeah," Virginia answered with a smile of her own. He stood up and dusted off his pants, then lowered his hand to help Virginia up. Still holding his hand for balance, she tip-toed up the bouldered incline until she regained her footing.

When they got back to the ferry area she turned to him. "See you tomorrow?"

"Sure," he said, apparently appreciative and a little amazed that she would want to see him again after what he'd told her.

With a last smile and a nod, she reluctantly made her way down the ramp to the ferry.

Virginia got up onto the deck and stared out at Tristan's little blue truck sitting on the shore. Even when the ferry began to move, she kept her eyes on the car until it disappeared from sight.

The wind blew threw her smooth brown hair as she stared at the bright, sparkling water beneath her. It was hard to believe that she'd ridden this same ferry only yesterday morning.

It seemed like a lifetime ago that she'd made this crossing. So much had changed since then and yet, when she looked around her at the water, the birds, the little green islands dotting their way, everything looked exactly the same.

The things around her hadn't changed. No. She'd changed. Something inside her had changed. Something was prompting her, more fully than ever to listen to the feeling in her heart. The tugging that told her she couldn't be comfortable anymore. The tugging that told her, after this weekend, she couldn't go back to life as it was. Life was too short, to precious to waste time being half-happy.

She knew the tugging came from God.

And, what's more, she knew that she had to follow her aunt's advice. She had to listen to it. She had to let go and follow where God led.

It had taken a car accident to make Tristan listen to the prompting in his heart. And she knew that if she didn't follow God now, it might take something equally drastic to change her. Well, she wouldn't wait for that to happen.

As the ferry pulled back into the dock where her car was waiting, she knew what she had to do. Things in her life had to change. Things between her and Jason had to change. She wanted them to change. Yet the looming fear hovered over her that if he wasn't willing to make that change with her, she'd have to make it alone.

Chapter 11.

It was late afternoon when Virginia made her way back home on Sunday. She had spent the entire car ride from the dock parking lot back to her duplex rehearsing in her head what she was going to say to Jason.

She couldn't ignore her heart anymore. The pastor had been right. If she was ever going to be happy, truly happy with Jason, then things in their relationship needed to change. She couldn't keep cooking for him, cleaning up after him, laughing off his jabs about her weight or watching him flirt with other women.

If this relationship was going to last, he was going to have to make a commitment. A real commitment to her. And that meant he was going to have to start doing some of the work.

As she pulled into her driveway, she had decided exactly what she needed to say. A surge of pride came over her as she walked up to the front door and unlocked it.

The feeling disappeared entirely when she saw what was inside her house.

It was a complete mess.

Empty beer bottles stood on nearly every empty surface. Two empty and crust-scattered pizza boxes lay next to each other in the living room.

As she walked from the hallway into the family room adjoining the kitchen, Virginia felt a tremor of fear pass over her. Maybe someone had broken in while she was gone. Maybe they'd been robbed.

However, when she glanced at the television in the living room, she noted that it was still there. So was all their stereo equipment, as well as Samantha's laptop computer which she always kept downstairs.

Virginia was confused for only a moment before she saw the pile of dirty clothes on the family room couch. She knew at a glance who they belonged to. As she moved towards them, she noticed the little note placed on the coffee table that confirmed her suspicions.

"Got home early from the business trip so I invited a few friends to hang out at your place," the note written in Jason's handwriting said. "I knew you wouldn't mind. Hope you had fun on your girl's camping trip! If you get a chance, could you wash the clothes on the couch? The washing machine in my apartment's out again.

Thanks,
Jason"

Virginia read the letter several times over
trying to comprehend the new low to which
her boyfriend had sunk. She knew he could be
a little inconsiderate. She knew that he
sometimes said or wrote things without
thinking, but this, coming over when he knew
she wouldn't be there. Not bothering to ask
whether or not she was alright with it. Inviting
other people to her house and then leaving it a
mess for her to clean up...this was a new low
even for him.

Cursing Jason in her mind, cursing herself
for letting him get away with this type of
thing, she crumpled the note and threw it in
the trash. She knew now that she would
seriously have to amend the talk she was
going to have with him. It was no longer going

to be a talk to try and fix their relationship. No, it was going to be a talk about ending their relationship.

She moved back to the couch and began to pick up the beer bottles on the coffee table. As she did, something lying between one of the cushions of the couch caught her eye. Trying to be sure of what she was seeing, she moved in closer to inspect it.

Sure enough, there, contrasted against the red fabric of her couch was a lacy black thong. What's more, without question, the skimpy little piece of underwear certainly hadn't come from Virginia's closet. And she knew her sister's wardrobe well enough to know that it hadn't come from Sam's either.

There, staring at a foreign piece of woman's clothing, Virginia finally admitted what she'd refused to see for years. Jason had cheated on her.

Maybe with the pretty little sales assistant,

maybe with someone else. Maybe it had happened once, maybe it was an ongoing thing. But there was no denying it now. Not with the evidence right here in front of her, clear as day.

She stood looking at the skimpy piece of fabric for several moments, feeling the anger and betrayal and rage well up inside of her. Then, marching to the pantry on the other side of the kitchen, she grabbed an empty cardboard box.

Taking it into the family room she threw all of Jason's clothes, along with the thong and all the beer bottles she could fit into the empty box. She had to get another box for the rest of the beer bottles, paper, and pizza boxes.

By the end of the night, she'd stormed through the house making sure that nothing of his remained. All of the books he'd left at her home, his movies and various sales papers were stuffed unceremoniously into the same boxes as his dirty clothes and garbage.

The next day, she woke up early and packed each box into her car. Once that was done, she scribbled a handwritten note of her own.

"Jason, it's over. Here is everything you left at my place including your black thong. Don't come over again. Don't call me. Don't try to see me at all.

-Virginia"

Taking the note in hand, she made her way to his television station. Placing the note inside the top box, she marched inside just as the doors opened.

Her smaller than average frame was fully covered by the boxes and from the corner of her eye, she could see people staring and pointing at her. She didn't care. In fact, she was surprised to find that she liked the attention she was getting from this little stunt.

She reached the station's sales desk and

plopped the boxes down in front of the sales assistant whose eyes widened at the sight of both her and the boxes.

"Are...are you here to see Jason?" the girl asked timidly.

"No," Virginia answered. "I don't want to see him. Just let him know that I dropped these boxes off for him. And, if he has questions, tell him to read the note."

Without another word, Virginia turned on her heel and made her way determinedly back out of the sales office. People in the hallways still occasionally stared at her and whispered behind their hands, but she paid them no mind.

Instead, she focused on marching to the front of the building and straight out the door. It was only when she got back into her car that the shaking started. She didn't know if it was brought on by rage or happiness or freedom or fear. But, it was there.

She took her hands off the wheel, sat back and tried her best to process what had just happened.

Virginia couldn't believe she'd actually done it. She left him. Her chest heaved and felt tight, but also free in a way she had never felt before. It felt as if the weight of the world had been lifted off of her. She was sad and freaked out, but also, dare she say it, excited.

An entirely new world was open to her now. There was no one left to tell her what she could and could not do. She wasn't attached to anyone else's dreams or plans anymore. Now, she could do exactly what she needed to do for herself.

It was still terrifying. She hadn't been on her own since high school. Along with the exciting possibilities came a crushing sense of responsibility. There were a million things she would have to do now. Decisions she would have to make for herself that she had never made before.

That was not to mention the deep hurt she felt everywhere inside when she thought about Jason. They had been together for so many years. He had cried with her when her mom died. He'd helped her with Aunt Emily as well. And now...all that was over. The chapter of her life where she'd had a strong, capable boyfriend, the kind she'd dreamed about her entire life, was gone.

This unfamiliar mix of sorrow, excitement, and fear left her paralyzed for several minutes. She sat in her car staring down at the wheel as though not quite sure what to do with it. Finally, she felt that tug in her heart again. And, this time, she knew exactly where it was leading her.

Chapter 12.

When she arrived at the island, she was surprised to see two cars waiting for her at the cottage. One was the familiar sight of Tristan's little blue truck and the other was Amanda's sedan.

Curious, Virginia put her car in park and moved towards the house.

"Of course we'll still need to put some new door knobs on before we show it," Amanda was saying to Tristan. "But, overall, it looks amazing. Virginia's going to be really happy."

"What am I going to be happy with?" Virginia asked walking up the steps to the front door. Both Amanda and Tristan jumped slightly and turned around.

"Oh! Virginia! There you are!" Amanda said moving down to greet her. "Tristan called me and said the house was just about finished. I thought I'd come up and take a look."

Virginia glanced over Amanda's shoulder at Tristan who was smiling apologetically at her.

"I know you still wanted to do some finishing touches," he said. "But, after you left on Sunday I came up and worked on the rest of main punch list. So, that's all finished."

"Oh," Virginia said. She wanted to feel happy and proud of what they had done, and she did. Still, she'd expected to be there when they decided the house was ready for Amanda to see. She supposed she'd imagined that, after all the work she and Tristan had done on the house together, there would be a special moment between just the two of them where they took it all in.

Apparently, that wasn't what Tristan had in mind.

"I'm...I'm glad you like it," Virginia said trying to keep her voice light.

If Amanda noticed anything amiss, she gave no sign of it. Virginia did notice when she passed Tristan, he was giving her that narrow-eyed appraising look that he got when he thought she wasn't exactly telling him the truth. She looked up at him and smiled, hoping to relieve his worry. He smiled only tentatively back at her and stepped aside to usher her into the house.

They toured the entire cottage top to bottom. As they went through each room, Virginia tried to listen to the mostly gushing praise that Amanda was giving to the woodwork and the furniture. -"Oh, that pine looks absolutely stunning on the deck!…I'm so glad you were able to move that wall out…The whole kitchen looks so much bigger". But she found that her mind couldn't focus.

Instead, as she moved through the house, she found herself bombarded once again with memories. Unlike the first time she'd come to the house, these memories weren't just of her aunt and her sister and her childhood. They were fresh from the past few months. When they walked through the kitchen, she smiled as she remembered the first time she'd torn down a wall with Tristan. As they moved through the family room, she remembered sitting next to Tristan on the couch just two nights before, laughing at a stupid silly movie. When they walked through the deck, she remembered Tristan's stories about building tree houses with his dad. When they moved to the yard she looked at the spot where she'd found the old key to her diary. The one that was now in a jewelry box up in the attic.

She wondered if she should have kept the key. Then she wondered what on earth she would have done with it.

Finally, they made their way out of the house and back to the front where Amanda's car was parked.

"Well, I'm sure we'll be able to get a really good offer on this place," Amanda said. "It's so charming and cozy! In fact, it looks better than it did years ago! And I love the artwork on the walls. Where did you find it?"

"You've got Virginia to thank for that," Tristan said. "We found some of her earliest paintings in her aunt's old boxes. So, we thought we'd hang them."

"You did those?" Amanda asked, looking to her in surprise.

"Yeah," Virginia said looking down at the

ground and feeling her cheeks grow warm. "I just...well...we didn't want to have to spend more money for art to hang around the house so, we used those."

"Well they're very nice," Amanda said. "Would you mind if I sold a few of them along with the house? I know a couple of my clients would love to have those prints hanging up. Gives the whole place an authentic feel. I'd pass the money on to you, of course."

Virginia blinked at Amanda trying to decide if the agent was being sarcastic or kind. Amanda looked back at her, apparently very serious about the prospect. Even so, it was a few moments before Virginia was able to answer.

"Um...yeah. Yeah. Of course," she said.

Tristan and Virginia said their goodbyes to Amanda and watched in silence as the sedan made its way back down the hill. As soon as the car disappeared, a tension began to fill the air between them.

"Ok. What's wrong?" Tristan asked turning to Virginia.

"What makes you think anything's wrong?" Virginia asked. Though, she knew that the way she was looking down at the ground and fidgeting with the sleeve of her shirt told him that she was lying.

"I thought you'd be happy about Amanda coming to see the place," Tristan said. "But, you didn't seem excited at all."

She looked up at him and his eyes were searching. There was no use trying to lie to him anymore. No point in trying to pretend to be happy about selling the house.

"I just...I just wish you'd called me or something to tell me she was coming," Virginia said weakly.

"I'm sorry," Tristan said. "I kind of wanted to surprise you. I worked all night Sunday to get everything finished I..."

He trailed off and looked away, averting the slightly rejected look on his face.

"...I thought you'd be happy. That's all."

The way he now turned his eyes to the ground and looked sideways caused a guilty knot to form in her stomach. After all, he'd tried to do something nice for her by finishing the house before she came out this morning. Which really was a very sweet gesture. She would have been thrilled if it were not for Jason and all the rest of it.

"I'm not unhappy with it Tristan," she said gently. "This was really nice. And you did a great job. I'm just...I'm a little upset with other stuff going on right now."

"What other stuff?" he asked looking up at her concerned.

She looked at him and knew she should tell him. After all, he'd been so open with her about his past yesterday. And it would be good to have someone to talk everything out with. But, when she looked into his bright blue eyes and saw his lips formed into a slight frown, the wind blowing in his curly hair, she wasn't sure how she could talk to him about Jason. Truth be told, she wasn't sure how exactly to talk to Tristan about another man at all.

"It's...it's a long story," she said. To her surprise, he smiled and rolled his eyes at her.

"I tried that with you just the other day as I recall," he said. "You wouldn't let me get away with it. Now, I'm not letting you get away with it either."

She smiled weakly and looked down once more at her hands.

"I just...I don't really know where to start," she said.

"Let's go inside and start with tea," he said holding his hand out to her. "My mom always said, no matter what the problem is, tea can make it better."

Though she wasn't quite sure if she believed his mother's old adage, she smiled anyway and took his hand, strong and warm in hers, and allowed him to lead her through the house to the kitchen.

It turned out that the tea helped. As they sat there sipping on what Tristan called 'Lady Grey Tea', which was a kind of sharp black tea with notes of orange in it, Virginia found herself telling Tristan the whole story.

She began with thinking about his pastor's sermon on the ferry ride home, rehearsing a conversation to have with Jason. Then, she told him about finding the mess when she arrived back at her house.

When she told him about the thong, she was surprised to feel tears begin to prick her eyes. That hadn't happened before. Even when she first found the underwear. She was upset, of course, angry even, she felt betrayed, but she hadn't cry. Now, however, she found tears pouring down her cheeks even as she tried to wipe them away.

Finally, she managed to finish that part of the story. Then she told him about the boxes and the note she'd written and put inside one of them.

He laughed at the image of her marching through a TV station piled with boxes of garbage and dirty clothes. To her surprise she laughed too.

"So, what happens now?" he asked gently.

"Now, I ...I don't know," she said. "I haven't been alone in a long time. It's kind of scary. But, I was thinking...I was thinking about not selling the house after all."

"Really?" he asked leaning over towards her from his chair beside hers at the kitchen table. He seemed eager. Almost as though he was trying to force down his excitement.

"Maybe," she said reluctantly. "I don't know. Everything seems just really up in the air right now."

"I can see that," he said. She looked up at him and he gave her a fortifying smile that she couldn't help but return. As she looked at him, she thought about everything he'd done for her so far. Not just finishing the house, but listening to her problems so non-judgementally, letting her come up to help even though he probably could have done the job more quickly without her, shopping with her, taking her to church... And, she'd never thanked him for it. Not properly anyway.

"You're...you've been a really good friend Tristan," she said. "Through all of this...everything, I mean. With the house and me and...I don't know how I would have gotten through the past few months without you."

That adorable pink tinge came into his

cheeks and he gave her another infectious smile.

"For what it's worth, the feeling's mutual," he said.

"I don't know how much I did, to help" Virginia said, feeling blood rush into her cheeks now as well. "I mean, you probably could've done it a little quicker without me."

Tristan smiled and rolled his eyes at her.

"Come on now," he said. "We both know that's not true. You turned out to be the best wall smasher in Washington. Possibly in the country."

They both laughed at the memory. When the laughter subsided, he moved his hand over hers resting on the table. Her heart beat began to speed up when she felt its warmth on top of her skin.

"But, it's more than just the house," he said. "I've...I'm really, really glad I got to know you."

Virginia tried to say that she was glad she got to know him, too. Yet when she opened her mouth to say it, the words wouldn't come. She and Tristan had leaned close to each other at the table. So close that she could feel the warmth of his breath on her cheeks.

Her pulse jumped into her ears as her mind told her that this was a bad idea. Whatever she was about to do. She'd just broken up with Jason. She needed time. She pushed the voice aside as she moved closer to Tristan and closed her eyes.

She felt his lips touch hers. It was a brief kiss. No more than a moment. After that, she heard his chair scrape back from the table and he stood up.

"Sorry," he said quickly moving to the kitchen door and looking away from her. "I...I shouldn't have done that."

Virginia felt her heart fall in her chest as she looked away from him as well.

"We both did it, Tristan," she said. "It wasn't just you."

"Yeah, but I...I've been..." he couldn't seem to finish the sentence. She wanted to ask him what he'd done, what he'd been thinking about her. About them. But, with Jason still swimming around in her thoughts, she couldn't quite bring herself to ask him that.

So instead she let the silence rush over them. They both stayed in the kitchen, him standing by the window, her seated at the round wooden table, neither looking at one another. The two cups of tea sat mostly finished in front of their seats. Virginia felt as though she should pick them up and put them in the sink. If only to have something to do with her hands.

In the end, she couldn't move even that much. After what seemed like hours but was probably only minutes, Tristan spoke.

"You should call your boyfriend," he said.

Virginia finally turned to look at him in shock. Of all the things she'd expected him to say after what had just happened, this was the very last.

"You mean my ex-boyfriend?" she asked.

"He's not your ex until you've talked things out," he said. "I mean, you haven't heard his side of the story. Maybe there's an explanation. Maybe he's sorry."

"I don't care if he's sorry," Virginia said angrily. Though she wasn't sure anymore whether that anger was directed at Jason or Tristan. This time she thought it was both. "I never want to see him again."

"But, see? That's the problem." Tristan said finally turning towards her. "You can't just end a long relationship like that with a note and an angry whim. You've got to talk it out. At least get closure, if nothing else."

A tiny part in the back of her mind knew that he was right. The rest of her was so angered by what he was saying to her that she couldn't admit it. She glared at him, still in her seat arms folded across her chest.

"So, you think I made a mistake dumping my cheating ex-boyfriend?" she asked.

"I...I don't know," Tristan said. "Maybe."

He looked down at his feet and a blush returned to his cheeks. It was the first time since she'd seen it that she didn't find it at all cute. In fact, she wanted to smack his cheeks so hard that they turned red instead of pink.

"I see," Virginia said gritting her teeth in anger as she stood up from her seat. "So, you've got this little boys code and you want to make sure you're not taking another man's property, is that it?"

"What?" Tristan said looking up at her shocked. "No, that's not-"

"Well, I'm not property," Virginia said. "I can make my own decisions and to tell you the truth, I'm getting pretty sick of men in my life trying to make them for me!"

She grabbed her purse and, for the second time that day, turned on her heel and walked purposefully toward the building's exit.

"Virginia! Wait!" Tristan said following her outside. "I didn't mean-"

"I'll come back some time next week to get the keys from you," she said ignoring his protests. "Your check will be in the mail."

With that she headed off down the path towards the dock. She heard him call after her several times but didn't dare turn back. Half of her expected him to follow her down the path to the ferry. In fact, half of her wanted him to. But, the further away she got from the house, the more she realized that he hadn't followed her. He'd given up.

For the second time that day, tears began to fill her eyes. This time, she made no attempt to wipe them away.

Chapter 13.

"Packages have been coming for you all day," Samantha said as soon as Virginia opened the door.

After she left Tristan on the island, she'd spend the rest of the morning and most of the afternoon driving around aimlessly. She didn't know where she wanted to go or what she wanted to do. The only thing she did know was that she didn't want to see either of the men who had caused her this much pain.

"I've got a kitchen filled with flowers, two boxes of chocolates and something wrapped in a box with little hearts. Don't tell me you've got a rich guy on the side you've been keeping secret."

Samantha, smiling, raised her eyebrows slyly at her sister as she led Virginia into the kitchen where there was indeed a table filled with a dozen red roses which Sam had put in a vase, two boxes of heart shaped chocolates and a thin package that had a note attached.

"Did any of these come with a note?" Virginia asked.

"The package did." Sam said. "I didn't look at it."

Her heart quickened as she lifted the note on the wrapped parcel. She found herself hoping against hope that it would be from Tristan. Even though she knew that was impossible. Not only were big gestures like this not his style, but she'd only left him that afternoon. He wouldn't have time to put all this together.

She knew that in terms of time, Jason was a much more likely candidate. However, she'd never gotten anything like this from him before. She'd never gotten even more than a single rose and a bag of Hershey's kisses from him for Valentine's day.

Sure enough, when she lifted the covering note on the package, Jason's handwriting stared back at her.

"My dearest Virginia," it began. "I know you said you didn't want to hear from me. And, just like you asked, I didn't come over and I haven't called. But I had to find some way to tell you how incredibly sorry I am. I know I've been a jerk and I know after what I did this weekend, I don't deserve for you to take me back. But I've done a lot of thinking today. And the one thing I know is that I can't lose you. I really want to see you so we can talk this out. More than that, I'd like to cook you dinner for once. You don't have to say yes or no. If you don't want to see me, I understand. But, if you would like to talk about everything, I'll have dinner for two ready at my apartment tomorrow night at seven o'clock. I hope I'll see you there.

All my love,

Jason."

Virginia stared at the note in her hands. It was different, so very different from the last note he had left her that she had trouble believing they were written by the same person.

Here he was open and vulnerable, almost pleading. Here, he apologized. She didn't think she'd ever heard Jason say he was sorry before. Not, at least, without qualifying it. But, here, he genuinely seemed to mean it.

Carefully, she set down the note and opened the package. Inside was a blank sketchbook along with a set of pencils and charcoal she'd pointed out to him at an art supply store months before. She'd told him that seeing it made her want to get back into drawing.

He'd scoffed at her then. Said that drawing would take her time away from the things that actually made money, baking, and teaching. But, now, here it was. He'd bought her something that he thought was impractical. Just because she'd wanted it. And even more than that, he'd remembered.

It seemed as though every issue, everything she'd wanted to talk to him about, everything she'd wanted to make him realize was either written in the note or set before her in the sketchbook and pencils.

As she stared between the note and her table filled with presents, she felt the hot anger that had spurred her on early that morning begin to melt away. She remembered all the times Jason had made her laugh, the times he'd seen her cry and held her, the times he'd helped her through the most difficult parts of her life.

These memories seemed to merge with the memory of that little black thong, and years of cooking for him and doing his laundry and paying for his graduate school. The two started to become so tangled in her mind that she didn't know how to untie them. She simply stood, sketchbook in hand, staring down at it blankly.

"So? Who's it from?" Sam asked. Virginia started at her sister's voice and seemed to wake from her stupor.

"Oh, they're from Jason," Virginia said. "We...we kind of had a fight."

She hadn't told her sister about the mess she'd found when she came back home

Sunday. The boxes with Jason's garbage were packed before Sam came back from the camping trip. Virginia knew even right after it happened, that if she told Sam that she thought Jason had cheated on her, Samantha would fly into a rage. She'd probably have marched right down to Jason's apartment and punched him until he bled.

No matter how angry Virginia had been at Jason, she didn't think he exactly deserved her sister's wrath. Even by simply mentioning the fight, Virginia could see her sister look up eagerly.

"Did you break up with him?" Samantha asked, unable to disguise the hope in her voice.

"I...sort of did," Virginia said. "I just...I just needed some time away. To think."

"And this is his way of trying to get you back?" Sam said giving an undignified snort to the gifts laid out on the table.

"I guess it is," Virginia said.

"So, are you going to?" Sam asked. "Take him back, I mean."

Virginia turned to Sam and saw her sister's pointed look. Sam's arms were crossed over her chest and her eyes were squinted at Virginia in an almost threatening way. She knew what Sam wanted her to say. She wanted her to say that Hades would have to freeze over before she would ever take Jason back. Samantha wanted Virginia to tell her that she was done with pretty boy forever.

But Virginia knew that she couldn't tell her sister that. Even though a part of her wanted to. The truth was, given the note Jason had sent, not to mention what had happened with Tristan on the island, she had no idea what she wanted at all.

All she did know was that she was going to have to figure it all out for herself. She couldn't let anyone, including her little sister, make her choices for her anymore.

"I don't know," Virginia said honestly. "I'm...I'm going to take a walk. Think about it a little bit."

Without turning back, Virginia took hold of the sketchbook, pencils, and charcoal and moved out the door. Once outside, she wasn't one hundred percent sure where to go.

There was a little park with a swing set down the street, and she walked absently until finally, she decided that she would go there.

It was nearly deserted by the time she arrived. The sun was setting in the distance, and she could see it sinking down over the distant waters of the bay. Even with the little wooden swing set in the way, the view was quite lovely.

Without thinking, Virginia took a pencil, opened her sketchbook and began to draw.

As her hand moved across the paper, she remembered something her Aunt Emily had told her about her drawings.

"God speaks to all of us in different ways," she said. "We feel closest to him when we're doing the things that we love to do. I think you feel closest to Him when you draw. I can see your prayer in your paintings."

Aunt Emily had been right about that. Virginia remembered many an afternoon sitting on the back deck of the little cottage, looking out into the woods and talking to God. They weren't the traditional types of prayers. Not the kind that started with Dear God and ended with Amen. No, she simply talked to God as though he were there beside her. As though talking to him was the same as talking to her mother or her sister.

It had been years since she'd prayed, really prayed to God that way. Now, as her hand moved gently across the paper, she found herself talking to God exactly the way she used to.

"God," she said silently. "I don't know what to do. I'm so torn. I don't know who to trust or where to go. I only know...or...I think I know that you've got a better way for me. You've got a plan for me beyond the life I've been living. You want me to use my talents for you and not to please my boyfriend or my sister or anyone else. I just wish I knew how to do that. Please, please show me."

She repeated similar words over and over in her mind as she carefully sketched the swing set and the view beyond it. The sun had almost set now and the sky had turned from bright orange to deep pinks and purples. The last rays moved slowly down over the water.

Looking out at that water, she couldn't help but think of Sweetwater. And, of course, thinking about Sweetwater made her think about Tristan. Now that hours had passed since the argument she'd had with him, now that her anger had subsided, she could see why he'd pulled away from her. She could see why he'd told her to talk to Jason.

He didn't want to be someone she turned to only because she was upset. Someone she could use to get back at her boyfriend. And, truth be told, that was what she had been doing.

When she kissed him, she was upset and vulnerable and thinking with her anger more than any other part of her mind. Now, the wisdom in Tristan's suggestion seemed to come through.

He was right. She needed to talk to Jason. Maybe she wouldn't take him back, maybe she would tell Jason that it was over for good. Maybe they would be able to work through things together. But, no matter what happened, she had to see him.

As the last ray of light moved down beyond the pacific, a little tug in her heart told her that she was on the right path.

So, as she made her way home, she pulled out her phone and typed "Dinner with Jason @ 7pm" into her calendar for the next day.

Chapter 14.

Virginia pulled up to Jason's apartment building still dreading what she would find on the other side of the door.

Half of her still protested the idea of seeing him at all. Indeed the part of her that hated confrontation insisted that she run away and speak to Jason only via email or text. But another part, the bravest part of her, told her that she needed to do this. Not for Jason, but for herself.

So, with a steadying breath, she walked out of her car, walked up to his apartment and knocked on the door.

"Virginia," he said opening the door. The widest and most heart-melting smile she had ever seen on him greeted her. He looked both surprised and ecstatic that she had actually accepted his invitation.

His hair had been combed, he'd shaved that five o'clock shadow and he was wearing his best suit. He'd clearly gone to a big effort and it was all she could do not to smile back at him.

"Come in," he said opening the door wider for her.

She entered the apartment without saying a word and without smiling.

His place really was tiny. It was a one bedroom efficiency about the size of most college dorm rooms. There was one small space between the television and sofa that made up the living area and the kitchen. This was where he'd set up a table and chairs complete with tablecloth and candles. Virginia also noticed her favorite jazz record was playing.

"Miles Davis?" Virginia asked in surprise.

"I know you think I don't remember this stuff," he said gallantly pulling out a chair for her. "But, I do. Believe me."

He allowed her to sit before moving to the kitchen to get the plates and what smelled like fettuccine Alfredo. Her favorite pasta dish.

As he came back to the table, she told herself that she had to applaud his effort. He poured her a glass of good red wine and they ate the first few bites of their dinner in silence.

Jason kept glancing up at her as though waiting patiently for her to start the conversation. Finally, she decided that she should indulge him.

"Jason," she started hesitantly. "My coming

here...it doesn't necessarily mean that we're going to get back together."

"I know that," he said, "but I figured, after everything I've put you through, I at least owe you a decent meal and a little pampering."

He gave her a charming smile and this time, she returned it weakly.

"This is really nice, Jason," she said. "So was the sketchbook you sent me and the flowers and chocolates. But...it doesn't make up for what you did."

"I know that too," he said. "And, for what it's worth, there's an explanation about that thong. But, I know you don't want to hear excuses from me. I know you don't want me to tell you how a bunch of this wasn't my fault. I know the truth is a lot of it was my fault. I've done a lot of things that I shouldn't have. I just wanted the chance to say I'm sorry."

He looked across the table at her, those hazel eyes that she had loved since she was sixteen years old, wide and pleading. He reached across the table and put his warm, strong hand on the top of hers.

"And I wanted to ask...do you think you could give us another shot?"

"Jason, I...I don't know," she said. "After so many years I just…"

"I know it'll take work," he said. The pressure from his hand, once soft and gentle became harder on hers. "I'm willing to put the work in, though. I've even gotten in touch with a couples counselor. She says she's got an opening on Friday if you'd like to go."

His hand was still hard on hers, his eyes were pleading and now desperate. It was like his life hung on her answer.

Virginia looked into his eyes and thought. On the one hand, this was exactly what she'd wanted from him. She'd wanted him to put effort into the relationship, to work not just for himself but for her, and more importantly, for them. Now, he said he was willing to do that. She looked in his eyes to find some hint of insincerity, some telltale sign that he wasn't serious. That he would break her heart again. She didn't see any.

So, with another steadying breath, she nodded.

"Ok," she said. "I'm...I'm finished with the house now so, I can make it on Friday."

With a relieved breath, Jason sighed, let go of her hand and leaned back in his seat.

"Good," he said. "Ok. I'll call her tomorrow and tell her."

Virginia gave him another weak smile and looked down at her fettuccine Alfredo, praying she'd just done the right thing.

"So, you're finished with the house?" Jason asked. "How is it looking?"

"Really good," Virginia said. "In fact, better than it did when I was a kid."

"Great," he said. "Does Amanda think

she'll be able to get a good price from it?"

Virginia's heart sunk in her chest. This one question reminded her so much of the Jason she used to know. The Jason she'd just broken up with. The one who was more worried about his bank account than anything Virginia wanted.

She knew that telling him she was thinking about keeping the house would put him on edge. And, what's more, if she and Jason were to get back together, if, eventually, they were to get married, she knew she would have to sell it anyway.

So, fighting against the horrible sinking feeling in her chest, she gave him a closed lipped smile.

"She saw it yesterday," Virginia said. "She thinks she'll be able to get more for it than she originally thought."

"Awesome!" Jason said. He flashed the cocky smile Virginia had come to know across the table at her. With some effort, she smiled back at him. They talked about some simpler things through the rest of dinner. Jason let her pick the show that they watched afterward.

When Virginia got into her car that night and made her way home, she knew she should feel less conflicted than she had been before going. After all, she'd done what Tristan had told her to do. She'd talked with Jason and they were going to try and work it out.

It had been Tristan, after all, who told her that it might have been a mistake dumping her boyfriend so hastily. Tristan who had pushed her to go back to Jason even though she'd fought against him. He had to have known that, if she did go back to Jason, she would sell the house.

Now, she realized, there was nothing left to resolve. She'd followed Tristan's advice and gone back to Jason. Everyone should be happy.

Even so, she still felt a tiny ebb of her heart pulling her in a direction different than the one she was taking. It pulled at her as she drove into her driveway and headed up the stairs to her bedroom.

In an attempt to ease her mind and, perhaps, silence the persistent, nagging feeling that she was making some kind of mistake, she got out her laptop and began an email to Tristan. She'd always liked emailing and texting better than calling. Less chance for confrontation that way.

"Tristan," she started.

"I've thought it over and I think I'm going to sell the house after all. Don't ask why, it's just something I've got to do. Thanks for all your help these past many months and I'm sorry about the way I left things the other day. I was upset and emotional. Just know that it had nothing to do with you. I'll be back to the island to pick up the key to the cottage sometime this week and I promise to put your payment in the mail tomorrow. You don't have to be there when I come to get the key. You can just leave it under the front mat.

Thanks again, for everything,
Virginia"

She stared at the message for several minutes, reading it over and over again, making sure it was exactly what she wanted to say. Her brain felt fried. She thought about telling Tristan about her and Jason; that he'd been right and they were going to work things out. But, in the end, it didn't seem to fit.

Finally, realizing she'd said all she needed to say, she hit send on the email.

She was still up in bed two hours later when the response came back.

It read:

"Virginia,

I guess I should say I'm sorry too. I'm sorry about the way I acted. You were right, I had no right to tell you what you should or shouldn't do about your boyfriend. But I have to tell you, I'm not sorry for kissing you. Truthfully, I wasn't even sorry when it happened, even though I said I was. Because, once it happened, I realized that I've been wanting to kiss you from the moment I met you. I know you probably don't feel the same way, but since we're being honest about so many things, I thought I should be honest about that, too.

I never set out to be anything other than a friend to you, but over these last six months so many things have changed. I've changed. And it even seems like you've changed; sometimes I think you glow when you show up at the cottage in the morning. I know that sounds ridiculous, but it's true. Maybe this project happened in order to help us both grow, I don't know. God's greater plan? Whose to say. But I think I would trust you with my life at this point. You are truly one of the best people I know. And not only at demolishing walls...

I really don't want to have to say goodbye to you via email. But, I also don't want to make the mistake of telling you what to do (again). So, I'll be at the cottage everyday this week., from nine in the morning until five in the evening. If you'd like to see me, come and drop the payment off then. If not, at the end of the week I'll leave the key under the mat. I really do want you to be happy, no matter what you do. Also, (one last bit of honesty), this isn't exactly how I planned to tell you this, but no matter what happens I want you to know, I am very much in love with you and always will be.

Love,

Tristan."

Her hand flew to her mouth. Virginia stared at the last two lines for what felt like hours. Her heart raced and for a minute she thought she might be having a panic attack, until she noticed that her cheeks kept creeping up into a crazy, disbelieving smile.

He loved her. Tristan loved her. The thought made her feel flush and excited and scared and numb all at once.

Then the reality of everything that had happened recently came crashing down on her and her thoughts started darting around wildly. Finally, because she didn't know what else to do, she closed the laptop, turned out the light in her room and laid back on her bed. Even so, she couldn't sleep. Tristan's words spun around in her head, interspersed with thoughts of Jason and all the recent events that had turned her world upside-down. In a desperate attempt at peace, she closed her eyes and fell into a fitful sleep feeling far more conflicted than she had been in as long as she could remember.

Chapter 15.

Friday finally came and Virginia grabbed the box of donuts she'd made along with her purse. When she turned to leave, she saw her sister standing in front of the door with her arms folded over her chest as though she was going to keep Virginia from leaving the house.

"Are you really sure about this Virginia?" Sam asked.

"I really am, Sam," Virginia said.

Samantha looked down at the floor and

shook her head.

"I still don't get it," she told Virginia.

"I know you don't, Samantha," Virginia said. "And that's what I love about you."

With a smile she reached across the tiled floor and pulled her little sister into a hug. The box of donuts got a little squashed by her side but, Virginia discovered that she didn't care.

"I'll see you later on tonight," Virginia said as Sam stepped aside to let her leave.

"Call me and let me know what happens," Sam called out to Virginia's retreating back. Virginia waved in response before getting into her car.

Setting the donuts on the passenger seat, she gripped the wheel, breathed deeply, looked herself in the eye and gave herself a pep talk. Then, she closed her eyes and prayed.

With only slight reluctance, she backed out of the driveway and headed down the road.

For eight-thirty on a Friday morning there was considerably less traffic than she'd expected, especially considering that with the arrival of fall, many of the schools were back in session. As soon as the car made its way out of her neighborhood, Virginia's phone vibrated. Spying her favorite coffee drive-through, she pulled into the line and let the car idle while she checked the message. It was from Jason.

"Something came up at work so I'm not going to be able to make the counseling thing today," it read. "You can go without me. I'll catch up at the next session."

Virginia blinked at the phone in disbelief. She read the message twice more. Though really she should have known better, she thought. No matter how hard Jason tried to show her another side to himself, no matter how often he said he couldn't lose her, he would always slip back into his old habits. He would always be Jason and, with a sigh,

Virginia realized there was nothing she could do about that.

The car line inched forward. Maybe she should go to the counseling session alone. The changes she'd seen both in herself and with the cottage since she started the renovation, were proof that a lot could be accomplished when you gave something proper attention. And she could now admit that before all this happened, Virginia had been the queen of putting everyone's needs before her own. She placed her order, noting that the Pumpkin Spice Lattes had finally arrived for the season. Veering from her normal tradition, she ordered an Eggnog Latte, another favorite of hers, but one that she usually forgot to order until it was too late and the season had passed.

Her mind kept playing through scenarios. Perhaps if she truly wanted to fix her relationship with Jason, she needed to not only keep working on herself, but incite the help of a professional. After all, no one is born knowing how to be in a relationship. She'd heard that somewhere recently. She supposed there was some truth in it. And people were constantly bemoaning how hard relationships were. Virginia had always felt like relationships shouldn't have to be as hard as people made them out to be. But maybe that was why she overcompensated in her relationship with Jason, she was trying to force it to be easy. Only problem was that she was the one it was taking the toll on. And admittedly it never felt as easy as she wished it did.

She pulled up to the window and got her drink. She smiled at the window attendant, finding appreciation that the simple things in life that could sometimes bring you peace. She dropped the change in the tip box and pulled out. She sipped her drink, the warm, frothy flavor instantly bringing her into the change of season. It reminded her of everything good, of being with her sister and bundling up to play in the leaves, of her parents, of her aunt, of walking to the cottage along the water and feeling strong, like she could do anything for the first time in so long. It was amazing, she thought, how something so simple as a smell or a flavor, could stir up so much.

Though she felt a little shell-shocked by Jason's text, she realized that she really didn't care in this moment. She felt a strange sense of contentment. Her body just wanted to drive, to sip her drink, to take in the beautiful mountains off in the distance, to breathe in the autumn air. She rolled down her windows and drove on autopilot. She passed the bay and glanced out the window to see people getting on the ferry for the islands. She continued on out of the city, taking the most scenic roads she could. The change of season was transitioning the leaves along the roadway from green to differing shades of brown and orange. When she had traveled this particular road as a child, she'd only ever driven it during the summer. But now, with the warm, comforting colors enveloping everything, it was even more beautiful than she remembered.

She drove for a long time, thinking that all that was ever asked of her was to follow her heart. Everything that she needed to know was being told to her. It was just a matter of whether she was open enough to listen to it. And she now knew that without a doubt, regardless of the outcome, she was ready to listen. That was all God asked of her. She was no longer afraid, and she trusted that wherever it led, was exactly where she was suppose to be.

She crossed over a rickety wooden bridge that looked as though it was patched and welded within an inch of its life. The water glittered just below it. Virginia mused that sometimes something phenomenal was just beyond something tattered and ruined. She smiled. She was feeling quite poetic today.

Tracing along the less familiar route, she made her way past the misty colored houses, with their endless charm and shingled roofs. Finally her car pulled to a stop at the top of the hill.

She nearly laughed out loud when she saw Tristan's truck parked in its normal spot.

Smiling broadly, she grabbed the box of donuts and rushed inside. There was no sign of Tristan in the kitchen or family room. But, she thought she knew where he might be.

She moved down the still slightly dark hallway towards the bedroom. The one she'd slept in when she was young. Sure enough, there he was. His back was turned towards her as he fit the new bronze knob onto her door.

"Going to work before breakfast?" she

asked slyly. "That's not like you."

He paused in his work and stood up slowly. He turned around.

When he saw her, his eyes lit up brighter than she had ever seen them. His entire face seemed to glow at the sight and she couldn't help but return his beaming smile a hundred times over.

"Virginia!" he said. "I...I take it you got my message?"

"Given the donuts that would be a safe assumption," she said still smiling at him. That adorable shade of pink came back into his cheeks but, this time, he didn't look at his feet. His eyes remained steadily fixed on her.

Neither of them spoke for several minutes, though her heart thumped so hard she was afraid he could hear it.

"Would you like to come into the kitchen?" Tristan asked. "I've got a pot of coffee brewing."

"Coffee and donuts," she said. "Sounds perfect."

They moved into the kitchen, box of donuts in Virginia's hand. She set them down on the counter and sat at the pinewood table while Tristan went to fill two cups of coffee. As she sat there, she couldn't help but look around at the house.

Taking in the furniture she'd bought, the beautiful shimmering new floors that Tristan had laid and best of all, her artwork on the walls. She couldn't help but feel that it was just what Aunt Emily always wanted.

Of course, it didn't look quite the way it did when Virginia was young. Not quite the way it did when Aunt Emily was alive. But everything looked like it fit here. It looked as though it was the same old house, ready for a new chapter of its life. And, Virginia thought, she was ready for a new chapter too.

"I've...um...I've got the key in here," he said

as he brought a coffee mug and set it down in front of her. "I guess you'll need to give to Amanda if she's going to be bringing buyers in to see it."

He was looking determinedly away from her as though he'd prepared himself for this. For her to say goodbye forever. For her to give up the house and everything they'd worked on together.

She reached out to him and, without hesitation, touched his hand. He looked up at her, his eyes shining with surprise.

"Actually," Virginia said. "I'm going to keep the house for a while."

"Really?" he asked, his face brightening again. She felt his hand turn from the table top and grip hers gently. "What made you change your mind."

"Will it sound silly if I say you did?" she asked sheepishly. "When I got your email, I realized that when you said you wanted me to be happy...I was happiest when I was here. In this house. To tell the honest truth...I was happiest when I was with you."

His eyebrows shot up at the realization of what she had just said. Then slowly, he gave her that narrow-eyed intense look that he got when he wanted to know the truth. He studied her for a moment, then, still silent, his other hand came up from the side of his chair and covered her hand as well.

He smiled up at her as he took his right hand back off of hers. He began fishing for something in the pocket of his jeans.

"I hoped you'd come back at least one last time," he said. "Because I made this."

He straightened up and held something small out to Virginia. Curious, she took it in her hand. Once she did, she realized what it was. A beautiful bronze ring with a tiny, shimmering jewel placed at the top.

"I know a lot has happened, and this isn't

much. But I couldn't let another bit of your heart get thrown away like your diary. That key is special to you...just like you are to me."

She looked down and saw the remnant of the tiny bronze key that had once unlocked her diary. The same one she'd put into the jewelry box and stuffed up into the attic. Somehow, he had worked the metal and fashioned it into an amazing ring like nothing she had ever seen before.

As she ran her fingers along the edges, staring in disbelief, he continued. "I know you might need to go live life and see what's out there, so I wholeheartedly want you to do whatever it is that's right for you. And I know we don't know each other well in the grand scheme of things, so I want you to take your time...but...when you're ready, if I'm the right person...and if you will take me, I want you to have this promise ring to know that I will be here waiting for you," he paused, shuffled his weight, then looked her straight in the eyes, "And I would be privileged to spend the rest of my life with you." Virginia wasn't breathing by this point, and when her eyes met his, she felt another deep tug at her heart. But this time she knew for certain that this one wasn't pulling her in any different direction.

"I mean, you don't have to take it now," he said looking back down and into his coffee cup, the pink coming back into his cheeks. "And, if you'd rather, I could just-"

She stopped him from saying another word by reaching across the table, putting both hands firmly on his warm cheeks and meeting his lips with hers.

This kiss lasted much longer than their first one had. Though, somehow, it seemed just as simple and every bit as sweet.

She didn't know who pulled back first. But when they did, they were both smiling.

"Is that a yes?" he asked.

"Yes, yes," she said chuckling. "Absolutely yes!"

With a chuckle of his own, he pulled Virginia back in to meet his lips again. And this time, when Virginia felt the little tug in her heart, she knew exactly what God was telling her.

She had taken a leap of true faith and was now, finally, on the path that was meant for her.

Epilogue.

Virginia was floating on air when she shared the news with Samantha. Virginia loved her sister so much and had hated not telling her everything that had been going on. At the same time, she was thankful she had been able to make the decisions that she had on her own.

The girls invited Tristan over to dinner in the city, and to Virginia's disbelief, he and Sam hit it off famously. They had a natural give-and-take with their humor and just had a really easy way with one another. The three of them ate dinner, played board games and laughed late into the evening. Virginia especially noted when all three of them worked together in the kitchen to clean up from dinner. Sam even gave Tristan a hug when he left. Life, Virginia thought, was definitely changing.

Sam was finally able to come out to see the house for the first time since the renovation. The girls spent the entire day running around, reliving memories in ever nook and cranny of the cottage. Sam couldn't believe what a transformation the house had gone through. "It's almost enough to make me want to live out on the island!" she had exclaimed. Later that day Sam told her sister, "Don't take this the wrong way. I love seeing you every single day, ridiculously so. But I have no doubt in my heart that this is where you belong right now. I'm really glad you did this." Watching the sunset just like they used to do when they were growing up, Sam punctuated her thought with, "Aunt Emily was a smart woman. This place is perfect, and I'm glad she knew that it was perfect for you." Virginia agreed, which prompted the girls to start shouting into the cool, amber-hued night, "We love you Aunt Emily! We miss you Aunt Emily! Thank you for everything Aunt Emily! I miss your corn bread Aunt Emily!..."

Virginia slowly started bringing personal belongings over to the cottage whenever she had a free day. She had decided to leave the downstair's room that had been hers as it was, and began spending more time setting up the large master bedroom. It almost felt like a right of passage, as if something had changed in her. She had grown out of the weaknesses of her youth, and moving into the upstairs room was a clean slate for the newer, wiser version of herself. It felt like the move Aunt

Emily had in mind. She was now the lady of the house, and Virginia had to agree that it suited her.

In just a few short weeks, she and Tristan fell into a regular pattern where Virginia would arrive on the first ferry of the morning and would be met at the dock by Tristan, who came armed with two ceramic travel mugs of coffee. They would walk as slowly as the morning dictated back to the cottage, talking about everything and anything that they felt like. The most recent discussions were about the future. These conversations were becoming so enlivened, that one day they sat on the back deck, where they usually ended up at the end of their walk, and made a decision. They decided that Virginia deserved to have proper closure on the last, very long chapter of her life. They wanted to be 100% certain that nothing they were doing was out of overly built up emotion from having an intense experience together…though they both secretly felt in their hearts that things were unraveling exactly as they were supposed to.

♥

Samantha and Virginia decided to plan an impromptu sister's retreat, just the two of them, so they could catch up on everything. They agreed that it was long overdue and it would provide the perfect chance for Virginia to have a little space to heal before moving on. They were lucky enough to take advantage of the last blip of good weather when they road tripped up to Vancouver, BC. They even made their way over to Vancouver Island, where they camped near the water and just focused on getting back to basics.

One day while sitting out overlooking the rolling tide, a lightness rose around Virginia. She looked out and watched the gulls commune along the sandy beach. She realized that the heavy burden that had lorded over her for so long had been swept away on a large Pacific gust. She felt so free being out from under Jason's oppressive personality and debts. Virginia looked out over the water and saw freedom, possibility and hope ahead. After grilling some local salmon over an outdoor fire one evening, the girls sat at the little wooden table and discussed it.

"What would you think if I just took a little time not teaching art and just figuring out what I want to do next," Virginia asked her sister. Sam look at her skeptically and Virginia felt a bit disheartened. After a few minutes of staring at her sister Sam leaned in and gave Virginia a look like she was an idiot. "Well duh! That's exactly what you should be doing," Sam chided. "Virginia, you are so much more talented and amazing than you give yourself credit for. What you do, or have been doing, is the bare minimum. You have so much more to offer the world and if you don't move out to the cottage and spend some time getting to know yourself again, and figuring out what you want to do next, I'll change the locks on the duplex and force you out…Or at the very least, I'll be super annoyed with you for at least two weeks." she looked up mischievously and threw her sister a wry wink.

They both fell into giggles, raised their white wine and clinked glasses. It did feel like a special occasion after all, a chance for them to celebrate new beginnings, sisterhood, and all the things that they had to be thankful for.

Virginia and Tristan had decided to try not to email or text during the time she was gone, which was really only made possible because there was zero signal where they were staying. They told each other that if they really felt the need to communicate, then they could write each other letters old-fashioned style, and they would exchange them when she was back. It had been a cute idea, and even Sam had to admit, a pretty romantic compromise. Now, Virginia found herself writing to Tristan almost every night. Not the long letters she had envisioned, but instead short, almost journal-like entries. She told him about her childhood and her family growing up, about her losses, her regrets, and even more so, she told him the dreams that she had been carrying around for so long.

The longer Virginia was away, the stronger her clarity grew about Tristan and the house and the need for a new direction in her life. At the end of the trip, she bound her journal-letters into a homemade book for Tristan. It didn't seem like life-changing information, but she was glad that she'd written it, as much for herself as to share with him.

The girls sang and talked the entire drive home. They made a game of stopping at every restaurant or rest stop that deemed itself "famous" on its roadside sign. By the time they re-entered the state of Washington, they had already ingested more crab, poutine, coffee, and fried dough than any one human should in a day. Samantha griped loudly about the hours she would have to clock in at the gym to undo all they damage they were inflicting, but then she would careen right back off the road as soon as she saw the next "world famous" sign.

When they finally arrived back home, Virginia found four letters hand-addressed to her mixed in among the bills and junk mail. That night she fell into bed, a cup of chamomile tea sat next to her reading lamp, and read. She felt like a giddy pre-teen with her first enormous crush. She couldn't remember the last time she had received a handwritten letter from someone, let alone four. Each one relayed some cute scenario that had happened to Tristan while she was gone. Something funny at church, the chaos that arose from materials for a job being on backorder, his poor assistant Ross's girl problems. It allowed Virginia to feel like she had been there the entire time, and she found herself giggling and reacting along as she read. The last one was her favorite, though. She traced her finger over the words as she read:

"While you've been gone, I thought about my entire life. Everyone I've known, everyone I've dated, all the situations I've found myself in, and I realized something. I feel weird saying this and don't know how to go about it without seeming too over-the-top or too...too much? Too soon? Just "too" everything. But sometimes you just have to blaze ahead regardless of embarrassment or potential disaster, so I'm going to say it (here on the safety of a piece of paper). I feel like, without a question, without a doubt, that you are the person I want to spend the rest of my life with. I have never been so certain about anything in my life. And I don't care if we don't have money or we don't have direction, but I know if we're together miracles will happen. So like I said before, take all the time in the world to heal, but know that I will be here waiting for you always. And I promise that I will always support you, lift you up when you're down & no matter what, I promise I will always be your friend."

When Virginia read that last line, her eyes welled. He had written so many cute, funny and loving things, but the idea that he loved her as a friend beyond anything else, struck her deeply in a way that she hadn't been prepared for. Somehow his saying that meant more to her than any grand gesture he could have done. Best of all, she absolutely believed him…and felt the exact same way.

Virginia arrived at the dock with a white box tied tightly with red twine. Making her way down the floating platform to solid ground, she quickly spotted Tristan over in the little grassy park with two paper coffee cups in hand. Once she got within 15 feet of him, impulse overtook her and she placed her box down on a nearby bench and ran at him full speed. He set down the tall paper coffee cups he was carrying just in time to catch her as she flung herself into his arms. They kissed for so long that Virginia started cracking up. Then she kissed him a little more for good measure. They walked through town so that Virginia could see the early efforts the town was making of putting up holiday lights. She had brought cinnamon buns from a popular bakery in Vancouver, and he had decided to surprise her with Eggnog Lattes for a change. They walked arm in arm through the little town that was now starting to feel very much like home.

When they stopped at a crosswalk, Tristan pulled her in close and kissed her temple. The warmth of his skin against hers, mixed with the smell of his shampoo filled her with a warm comfort. When the intersection was clear they began to walk again. The telltale tugging in her heart now felt more like tiny explosions. It was intense, and amazing, and she hoped she would feel it for a very long time to come. She looked up to the crisp blue sky with its stretches of perforating white clouds, and with all the appreciation in her heart, mouthed, "thank you."

ACKNOWLEDGEMENT

I have so much love and appreciation in my heart for my amazing family and friends. I could not imagine life without each and every one of you!

To my mother-in-law Julia: Thank you for being the initial inspiration for this part of my journey. You are the original muse, and I hope you know how loved you are. Your support, brainstorming sessions and late nights reading add light to my life and make this process so much more rewarding.

To my BFF Caroline: I could not, would not, be able to do this without you. You are the rocket fuel to my very talkative rocket ship, and my life is better because you are in it. To making our dreams come true!

To the illustrious Rachel: Your creativity and inspiration have been tantamount to this project! Thank you for all that you do! Like Virginia's tugging heart, I just knew instinctively that you were meant to be part of this team. You are endlessly appreciated!

To the love of my life Drake: I love you so much, even though you are the wackiest, most complex man I know. Thank you for tolerating my antics, helping to add a man's perspective to things, and for always doing the dishes.

To my parents: I love you more than words can say. Nothing I have ever done would be possible without you. You have supported me, loved me, guided me and rolled your eyes at my goofy nature. No girl on Earth is as lucky as I am. Thank you, from the bottom of my very full heart.

ABOUT THE AUTHOR

Sophie Mays is a contemporary romance author who focuses on inspirational stories with heartwarmingly happy outcomes. Believing that we are all put on this Earth with a purpose, no matter how big or small it seems, Sophie knows that without a doubt each and every one of our contributions is essential to making the world go round. After many years of writing, and doing a great deal of soul-searching on the side, she found that her contribution was the thing that was obvious to all...she was through and through, devoted to bringing hope, happiness and motivating inspiration to everyone around her. Whether through her books or her personal relationships, Sophie has always been known for her dogged dedication to making people believe that anything is possible if you truly believe and put your faith in up above.

Aside from being a full-time writer and optimist, Sophie maintains an impressive collection of magazines (piles of Southern Living and Real Simple are constantly being recycled by her husband), she is addicted to audio books, loves inspirational podcasts, and scours the globe (aka recipe books) in search of the perfect "healthy" dessert to bring to parties. She lives in the coastal South, where she feels lucky to get the best of both worlds: the sound of rolling waves, salty air, lemonade tea, and sweet Southern charm.

Visit www.LoveLifeFaith.com to learn more

42794784R00168

Made in the USA
San Bernardino, CA
10 December 2016